Short Stories One

Compiled by Roger Mansfield

Illustrated by John Dugan

SCHOFIELD & SIMS LTD., HUDDERSFIELD

0 7217 0300 3

0 7217 0330 5 Net edition

First printed 1977

Short Stories is a series of three books.

Book One	0 7217 0300	3
Book Two	0 7217 0301	1
Book Three	0 7217 0302	x

Printed in England by Garnett Print, Rotherham & London.

CONTENTS

ACKNOWLEDGEMENTS

The compiler and publishers wish to thank the following for permission to use copyright material:

Penguin Books Ltd., for 'Still Jim and Silent Jim' from 'What the Neighbours Did and Other Stories' by Philippa Pearce (Longman Young Books 1972). Copyright © Philippa Pearce, 1959, 1972.

Winant, Towers Ltd., for 'Vaarlem and Tripp' by Leon Garfield.

Faber and Faber Ltd., for 'A Haunted Terrace' by William Mayne from 'The Faber Book of Stories'.

The Save the Children Fund, for 'The Friday Miracle' by John Rowe Townsend and 'Tom Turnspit' by Barbara Leonie Picard, from 'The Friday Miracle and Other Stories'.

Mrs. George Bambridge and the Macmillan Company of London and Basingstoke, for 'Rikki-Tikki-Tavi' from 'Jungle Stories' by Rudyard Kipling.

Rigby Ltd. (Australia), for 'The Fish Scales' by Colin Thiele from 'The Rim of the Morning'.

Wm. Collins, Sons & Co. Ltd., for 'Forms of Things Unknown' from 'Of Other Worlds' by C. S. Lewis.

A. W. Sheppard, for 'Holidays' from 'The Nature of Love' by Judith Wright.

INTRODUCTION

The line between stories for adults and stories for children is an imprecise one. Some critics and writers have even suggested that no distinction can be drawn between the two. In terms of intrinsic literary quality, this argument certainly holds true. There is no reason why lower standards should apply to literature intended for children; no reason why younger readers should be satisfied with hackneyed plots, stereotyped characters, unconvincing action or trivial themes. There are, however, other considerations. Any reader must be able to respond to a book.

> One does not write *for* children. One writes so that children can understand. Which means writing as clearly, vividly and truthfully as possible.
>
> Leon Garfield

If a story goes too far beyond a reader's experience or imagination, or if the style and vocabulary present tedious barriers, there will be no communication. And if this happens too often, there is a real possibility that reading, as an enjoyable and worthwhile recreation, will be discarded. It is on these grounds that teachers, librarians and parents are justified in distinguishing between literature for children and books for adults.But to exaggerate the gap can be as dangerous as to ignore it.

> One does indeed write *for* children, but there isn't really any Great Divide.
>
> John Rowe Townsend

The aim of this series is to reduce the risk that younger readers themselves will see a Great Divide where none exists, to present stories that are both accessible and, at the same time, capable of widening horizons − stories that the reader will *always* enjoy, whatever his or her age.

> A children's story which is enjoyed only by children is a bad children's book.
>
> C. S. Lewis

Philippa Pearce

Philippa Pearce was born in 1920 in the Cambridgeshire village of Great Shelford, where her father was a flour miller and corn merchant. As children, she and her brothers and sisters spent many hours fishing, bathing and skating on the River Cam, which flowed along one side of the mill-house garden. They also had an old canoe in which they went boating.

Her first book, *Minnow on the Say,* is about two boys from very different backgrounds who, in an unusual treasure hunt, share just such a canoe on just such a river. Her second book, *Tom's Midnight Garden,* features the mill-house garden as it must have been in her father's childhood (he was born in the mill-house). In this outstanding story a boy goes to stay in an old house with his aunt and uncle. When the grandfather clock strikes thirteen at midnight, he goes to investigate, enters the garden and finds himself back in Victorian times. The "old days" also feature strongly in grandfather's conversation in STILL JIM AND SILENT JIM, which is set in a village not dissimilar to present day Great Shelford. Her other stories include *A Dog so Small,* about a working-class boy who has an imaginary chihuahua but who ends up with a real mongrel, and *The Strange Sunflower,* in which a boy dreams that he enters sunflower land. In 1963 she collaborated with Sir Harold Scott to produce a junior version of *Inside Scotland Yard.*

For thirteen years Philippa Pearce was a scriptwriter and producer in the BBC Schools Department. Since then she has worked in publishing and has edited a large number of books, including the social history series *People of the Past.*

Still Jim and Silent Jim

by Philippa Pearce

Old James Heslop came to live with his daughter-in-law when young Jim was still a baby. By then Mrs. Heslop was a widow with four children—young Jim being the last. She was glad to take in old Jim to live with the family. It was true that he overcrowded an already crowded little house, and—since he could not get up and down stairs—he had to have the downstairs room which had the television set in it. On the other hand, he gave his daughter-in-law nearly all his Old Age Pension, as his share of the housekeeping expenses. Besides, Mrs. Heslop, hard-worked and harassed and sharp-tongued even to her children, had a kind heart. "When you're old, you need a real home," she said. "This is Grandad's as long as he wants it."

Old Jim was less trouble than might have been supposed. Take the television set, for instance. He was not at all interested in watching television, but, as he was stone deaf, he did not mind the rest of the Heslop family having it on in his room. Indeed, as long as his chair was turned so that he need not look directly at the screen, he enjoyed it. "That makes a flickering on the walls, like firelight," he would remark. "And you don't always get the chance of an open fire to sit by these days."

Another convenience of old Jim's deafness was that he did not mind the noisiness of the three elder Heslop children; and of young Jim—who never said much anyway—he was very fond. It was a mutual affection. As soon as he could crawl, young Jim crawled round his grandfather's chair; and he first stood upright, rocking on unsteady legs, the better to listen to the deep, booming voice that was all the louder for old Jim's never hearing it himself. Young Jim listened before ever he could have understood what was being said; even later, he very rarely attempted a word in reply. In summer, old Jim's chair was put out into the front garden, and he sat in the sun, with his hands motionless on the rug over his knees, statue-like except for his jaw that moved when he spoke; and young Jim roamed about the flower-borders, listening but silent. That was how the pair got their nickname from the neighbours: Still Jim and Silent Jim.

Young Jim was so silent that the neighbours said privately that he must be simple-minded; but when he went to school he proved otherwise. He still spoke as little as possible, but he learnt as well as anyone.

Even before young Jim had learnt to read properly, he began bringing books home to show to his grandfather. The old man's eyesight was still good, and he read the text and looked at the pictures and told Silent Jim what he thought. Old Jim enjoyed books of history especially. He sighed and shook his head over them. "Ah! those days!" he said; and it cannot always have been very clear to young Jim whether those days had been his grandfather's, or days of long, long before his grandfather's birth. Old Jim pored over illustrations of the earliest motor-car and the penny-farthing bicycle, and before that the stage coach, and the pack-horse, and the Roman chariot—"Ah! those days— those days! And the men that lived then! Why, they were giants on the earth in those days!" The neighbours, overhearing the old man, would smile and tap their foreheads, for they were sure that if Silent Jim were not simple-minded, Still Jim had become so—at least, a little. The rest of the Heslop family did not believe it of their grandfather, but they paid no attention to him—that is, all except for young Jim: he listened closely, staring with eyes just the blue of his grandfather's but not yet faded with extreme age.

Old Jim had been over eighty when he moved into the Heslops' television room, so he must have been over ninety when young Jim was about ten. By then young Jim would occasionally—if necessary—start a conversation. One day he planted himself in front of his grandfather and said: "If you're over ninety, Grandad, you must be over sixty as well." He did not shout—that would have been of no use; but he used an oddly still voice that seemed to creep into old Jim's ears in a way that no bawling could have done. Besides, he stood where the old man could watch his lips, and he shaped them very distinctly in speaking.

"Aye," said old Jim.

"Then you could belong to the Over Sixties' Club up the village," said young Jim, and cocked his head at him. Old Jim cocked his head back, and they stared at each other for a while.

"There's a boy at school," said young Jim, "his grandad goes. They play dominoes, they do, and whist. They have cups of tea, they do, and birthday parties. It's in the Church Hall."

"How'd I get there?" said old Jim.

"Oh!" said young Jim, and stared and pondered, and at last wandered away. This was before the time that the eldest Heslop girl took up with nice young Steve from the garage, who could hire a car very cheaply for his friends.

A day or two later young Jim came to his grandfather and said: "There's bath-chairs that belong to the Over Sixties' Club."

Old Jim nodded, as though to congratulate young Jim on a fine piece of investigation.

"They cost nothing," said young Jim.

Old Jim nodded, and stared at young Jim. This time young Jim nodded back.

No more was said on the subject, but the following Friday young Jim wheeled a bath-chair up to the Heslops' house and as near to the front doorstep as it could be got. Then he went in to fetch his grandfather. Mrs. Heslop came running, in agitation. "Whatever are you thinking of, Jim!" she cried. "You're never going to get your grandad into that chair—not with his heart—not with his joints—not at his age!"

"I'm going to the Over Sixties' Club," said old Jim. He threw aside his rug and, with a stick in one hand and the other hand on his grandson's shoulder, he struggled up out of his armchair.

When old Jim stood up, you saw that he was a tall old man—"six foot, even allowing for shrinkage," he always said; and then would add: "And my father was well over six foot, and my grandfather—that lies in the churchyard over in Little

9

Barley—he was seven foot. You can see his tombstone there, like a giant's. Ah! those days!"

Now, seeing him determinedly on his feet, Mrs. Heslop cried: "And look at yourself, Grandad! You're a big, heavy man, even if you are skin and bone! Young Jim can never push you all through the village to the Over Sixties' Club!"

"I can," said young Jim.

Old Jim reached the bath-chair and let himself down into it; young Jim lifted his legs in after him, and put the rug over them. Then they set off.

"Anyway, you're to be careful!" Mrs. Heslop called after them. "You're to mind all that traffic on the London road!"

Great Barley, where the Heslops lived, was a busy, built-up village, with a main stream of traffic running through it on the way to London. "Not like the old days," said old Jim. "Great and Little Barley, they were both quiet then." Little Barley, being several miles away and quite off the main road, was still quiet. Hardly anyone went there.

Fortunately, to reach the Over Sixties' Club at the other end of Great Barley village, Silent Jim and Still Jim never had to cross the main road at all. They arrived safely.

The Chief Organiser welcomed them. She smiled in a kindly and congratulatory way at young Jim. "That must have been a long, hard push for a boy of your size. Now you must run off, and come back at five o'clock to take your grandfather home again. Children can't attend the Club."

Young Jim stared at the Chief Organiser, answered nothing and stood his ground. She said in a low voice to the other organisers, "I don't think he can understand." She turned to old Jim. "Your grandson——" she began.

Slowly he moved his hand up to cup it round his ear, and looked inquiring. "I'm deaf," he explained; "deaf as a post; deaf as a stone."

"Your grandson——" shouted the Chief Organiser.

Old Jim shook his head. "No, I shall never hear." He looked at her pleasantly. "But you mustn't think I'm unhappy. I'm very happy. If I have young Jim with me, I'm all right. Never you mind us."

11

The Chief Organiser gave up, and young Jim remained with his grandfather—the only child regularly to attend the Over Sixties' Club. He sat by old Jim, watching his play at dominoes, holding his saucer for him when he drank tea and picking the cake crumbs off his waistcoat. Young Jim himself drank tea and ate cake, but old Jim always paid for both of them, so that you could not say that the Club was cheated of anything. Moreover, young Jim kept the bath-chair (they always used the same one) in apple-pie order, brushing out the bottom, where old Jim put his feet, polishing the metalwork and oiling the little wheels in a vain attempt to get rid of their squeak. After a while, the Chief Organiser said the bath-chair might be kept in the Heslops' outhouse, which was done.

At about this time Maisie Heslop began her friendship with young Steve from the garage. He suggested that, one summer Sunday, he should take the family on a day's outing to the seaside; he would hire the car and drive.

All the Heslops went. Mrs. Heslop sat at the front with Steve, and Maisie sat between them—she did not seem to mind being squeezed up a little. The other three children travelled at the back; and right across the back seat, underneath them all, travelled old Jim. It seemed hard on the old man—it was hard for them, too, because he was very bony—but he found it was the only way he could go in a car at all. "That's not a patch on a bath-chair," he whispered to young Jim; but what old Jim thought to be a whisper was something quite loud and clear. Everyone heard it; and Steve laughed, and Maisie went red with indignation.

Old Jim had to get into the car before the others, because he had great difficulty in bending his back and legs. First of all, he sat backwards on to the seat, and some of the Heslops went round to the other side and leaned into the car and pulled him, and the remainder of the Heslops stayed at his legs end and pushed him from there.

Old Jim puffed and groaned. "That's not worth it," he said. "'Tisn't the way to travel—hemmed in—" (he knocked his head against the roof of the car) "—boxed down! That was different in the old days: carriages, and horses; room to move—fresh air! A bath-chair, now, that's a kind of carriage."

"You may like a bath-chair for some things," said Steve, "but it can't go as fast as a car."

"I've heard you say to young Jim that you wish sometimes he could push your bath-chair faster," said Mrs. Heslop.

"You'll never go anywhere farther than your old Club, just in a bath-chair. In Steve's car we shall get to the seaside and back in a day," said Maisie.

Young Jim said nothing, because he never did; and the other two Heslop children were too busy pulling and pushing.

Old Jim said nothing, because he had heard nothing.

By now old Jim was completely in the back of the car; but cross-corneredly, with his right elbow against the window of the right-hand door, his left elbow against the back window and his toes turned up against the bottom of the left-hand door. He was in—just.

Having made sure that the door could be shut on him, the three younger Heslop children opened it again and climbed in on top of their grandfather. They sat where they could. Young Jim sat on old Jim's stomach, because someone had to sit there, and he was the lightest. Also he was his grandfather's favourite.

So they set off. When they reached the seaside, old Jim was pulled out of the car and put into a deck-chair. He was so breathless from the journey and so exhausted from getting in and out of the car that he dropped into sleep at once. He woke up for the picnic, and again to be put back into the car. When they got home and they were all thanking Steve and saying what a good driver he was and what a nice car and what a pleasant trip, old Jim said loudly: "Never again!"

"Grandad!" said Mrs. Heslop reproachfully. "And after such a lovely day!"

"And Steve's having taken such trouble!" cried Maisie.

"Don't mind me," said Steve, for he really did not mind.

"They talk about modern improvements, I believe," said old Jim. "Some things are improvements; some aren't. Especially for people too old for them—or too big. I daresay I'm an old-fashioned size for travelling in a modern motor-car. What my grandfather would have done—he that was seven feet tall—broad, too——"

"It's not kind to Steve!" Maisie cried. "And I don't believe your old grandfather was seven feet high, so there!" And she burst into tears.

"What's she crying for?" asked old Jim. They all looked at young Jim to explain. He was silent, and Maisie went on crying.

"What did she say?" asked old Jim. "Nobody tells me anything nowadays; for some reason nobody speaks to me—except young Jim. Come on, Jim, you tell me what she said."

Young Jim looked uncertain, but he said: "She says it's not kind to Steve." Old Jim looked dumbfounded. "And she says she doesn't believe your grandfather was seven feet high, so there."

Old Jim put his head back, closing his eyes, as though he were too tired to speak. At last he said: "So that's what's behind it. They've never believed me. Everything's modern nowadays, and everybody's young and small; and they all believe that's the right thing, and the only thing, and that it was never any different. They don't believe in those old days."

"O Grandad!" said Maisie, and began crying in a different way. "I didn't mean that. Young Jim, tell him I didn't really mean that."

"Grandad!" said young Jim, and took the old man's hand and

14

shook it gently until he opened his eyes. "Grandad, she says she didn't mean it."

"They don't mean me to know what they think," said old Jim; "but they think it all the same."

There was nothing more to be said. Maisie went on crying for some time; but, on her mother's advice, she did not speak of the subject again.

The next time that Steve brought the car round to take the Heslops on a jaunt—to Whipsnade Zoo this time, to see the animals—old Mr. Heslop said he would stay at home. Maisie made him egg sandwiches for his tea, and kissed him good-bye remorsefully. Silent Jim stayed with him, although he, too, loved to see strange animals.

The summer advanced. Every Friday young Jim pushed his grandfather's bath-chair through the village to the Over Sixties' Club. Then the organisers decided to close the Club for the month of August, because most people went on their holidays then. The Heslops could not really afford a holiday; but Steve from the garage took Maisie and the two middle children off to a seaside camp for a fortnight. Mrs. Heslop did not go: she said it would be holiday enough to be left in the house with three less children than usual. Old Jim did not go, because he said he didn't want to; and young Jim would not go, even at his mother's urging. He would not say why, but his grandfather looked at him sadly: 'You'd have enjoyed the sea." Young Jim neither assented nor contradicted. "You shouldn't have stayed for me," said old Jim.

Young Jim thought that old Jim might be lonely; and old Jim worried that young Jim might be dull. Every day of that hot season the neighbours saw them out in the front garden of the Heslops' house, in what shade there was: Silent Jim busy with some job of his own making, and Still Jim talking to him. Since the time of his unhappy return from the day by the sea, the old man had not referred again to 'those days'. Now, however, alone with young Jim, he felt free to go back into his memory for stories to interest and amaze. He would always end by saying: "And that was true, for all there's nothing left to prove it, and people disbelieve."

One late afternoon he had been talking in this strain for some time. They had finished their tea; and young Jim had got the bath-chair out and was cleaning the wickerwork with an old toothbrush. Mrs. Heslop came out to fetch their tea-things, and said: "It's a pity there's nowhere to take your grandad in the bath-chair, till the Club opens again next month." She went in again to do the bit of washing up.

Old Jim had stopped talking, and he did not start again now. Young Jim looked up at him in surprise. His grandfather beckoned to him to come close. "If I speak like this," he said, "can anyone hear but you?"

Young Jim looked round carefully. There were no neighbours in the gardens, and his mother was in the kitchen with the taps running. He shook his head.

His grandfather put his hand up and pulled young Jim's head into such a position that the boy's ear was only a few inches away from his mouth when he spoke. "What would you say to a jaunt—a real pleasure-jaunt?"

Silent Jim turned his face so that his grandfather could see his eyebrows going up.

Old Jim nodded. "Mind you, it's a long push with the bath-chair."

Silent Jim simply left his eyebrows up.

"It came to me just now, in a flash," said old Jim. "The whole plan. We'll go over to Little Barley, where I was born, where I was christened at the font in the church there, with my father and grandfather standing by—my grandfather that's buried in the same churchyard—he that was seven foot tall. I'll show it to you—all of it."

Young Jim said: "When?"

"The sooner the safer, before the weather thinks to break. To-morrow; and very early in the morning, before the traffic's on the main road, at least for our first crossing of it; and before others are about. Before your mother wakes."

Silent Jim nodded emphatically.

"Sunrise is before five now," said old Jim. "I've often seen it, for at my age I sleep lightly, and never late."

It was easy for old Jim to wake early, but a different matter for young Jim; and it would be impossible for his grandfather to call

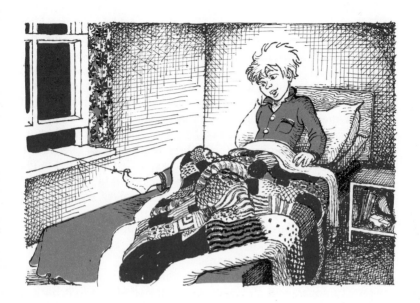

to him without waking Mrs. Heslop, too, or to get upstairs in order to wake him quietly.

Young Jim's bedroom upstairs, like old Jim's room on the ground floor, was at the front of the house. This gave young Jim his idea. That evening he made a very long length of string out of several shorter pieces knotted together. The string stretched from his bedroom, out through the window, down and in again at the window of his grandfather's room. The lower end was left within easy reach of old Jim's hand; the upper end was tied round young Jim's big toe. The device was put into working position after Mrs. Heslop had gone to bed; and the next morning—before morning seemed even to have come—it worked perfectly.

That summer dawn surprised young Jim by its stillness and greyness: he had expected at least reds and yellows in the sky, like a festival. He was surprised, too, at the chill in the air, even indoors, at this time of heat-wave. He dressed his grandfather in his warmest clothes, and gave him an extra rug for the bath-chair. They had not planned to have any breakfast at all, but now young

17

Jim—who was a sensible boy—saw they would need something later to warm them. The most that he dared do was to boil a kettle and make a thermos flask of tea. He also put a handful of digestive biscuits into a paper bag. "And," said old Jim, in his lowest voice, "we'll take your mother's tape-measure." He would not say why.

With old Jim in the bath-chair, and the flask and biscuits and the tape-measure on his knees, they left the house. In all the houses they passed the curtains were still drawn; none of the neighbours was up. Young Jim pushed the bath-chair along with his heart in his mouth, for the squeak of the wheels sounded very loud in the morning silence. Perhaps, if anyone heard at all, the hearer thought it was only the early, monotonous call of some strange bird.

They left the housing-estate and came out on to the main road. There was no traffic at all to be seen, until an all-night lorry rumbled by. Then nothing again.

They crossed the main road unhurriedly and without the slightest danger, and struck off down the road to Little Barley. Now that they were leaving the houses of Great Barley behind them, old Jim dared talk aloud; and young Jim, feeling that they were really on their way, relaxed his pace and looked around him as he went.

This was a country road, going always deeper into the country. There were wide verges where the grasses grew tall, yellowing and drying with the heats of August. There were few flowers left in bloom; but the plants in the ditches were fresh and green where they could still suck up refreshment and life from ditch-water or ditch-mud.

Dew lay on grasses and plants and hedges—a short-lived coolness before the sun should come again in its full strength. Already young Jim began to feel its warmth on his back; and bath-chair and bath-chair-pusher together began to make a strange long shadow on the road ahead.

They came to a bridge over a river and crossed it; they skirted a high wall—old Jim made young Jim stop to look at a fading black mark on it. When he was a young man, old Jim said, that mark had been repainted yearly: it was the boundary-sign between the parishes of Great and Little Barley. When he was a boy, the champion fighter of the two villages stood with a foot on either side of the mark and shouted:

> Barley Little and Barley Great,
> Here I stand and won't be beat.

They went on, and crossed a railway line, where you opened the gate for yourself and had to look both ways for safety.

They reached the outskirts of Little Barley village—a cluster of cottages and a farmhouse, and the church beyond. They still saw no sign of anyone astir and heard no sound of life, except a clank of metal from a farm-building—perhaps a bucket in a cowshed where the early milking was starting.

They came to the little grey church. Young Jim pushed the bath-chair up the path between the tombstones, to the church door. The door might so easily have been locked, but it was not. Young Jim could have wheeled the bath-chair right inside, but old Jim thought that it might not be respectful. He got out of the chair instead, and, leaning on young Jim's shoulder, he hobbled inside.

Little Barley was such a small village that no rector or vicar lived in it, and services were held in the church only occasionally. You could feel that on entering. There was a silence that was surprised to be disturbed. Church spiders had spun threads across and across the aisles, from pew-head to pew-head. Young Jim felt them breaking across his body as he and his grandfather paced along.

Now they were facing the east end of the church and the altar. Behind and above it was a great window of pale greenish glass, through which streamed the light of the risen sun.

Old Jim blinked into the light, and his eyes filled with tears, and he sat down rather suddenly in the pew beside him, and prayed.

When he had finished, he said to young Jim: "I was married to your grandmother at that altar. She died long before you were born." Then he took young Jim to the west end of the church, to the grey stone font. "I was christened here; my mother and father stood here for my christening. They're dead and gone, too."

"And your grandfather stood with them," said young Jim. "He that was seven foot high."

"Aye, and he's gone, too." But this reminded old Jim of

something. "I'll show you, outside," he said, "towards the east end of the church, it would be—his grave."

They went outside again, and, as old Jim was tired, he got back into the bath-chair and young Jim wheeled him along the narrow path that went round the outside of the church. Towards the east end of the churchyard, old Jim said, "Stop!" He looked round him. "You'll find it about here. James Heslop, his name was—like my name—like yours."

Young Jim began to look. The graves in this part of the churchyard were very old, overgrown and weatherworn. The inscriptions were hard to read.

Old Jim saw his grandson's difficulty. "Look for a big tombstone—the biggest. Seven foot tall he was, and his tombstone was to match."

"This is the longest tombstone," said young Jim at last. He scraped away the ivy tendrils from the head of it. "There's an O here—no, it's a cherub's face. But there's writing below. I can't read the first letters, but here's an S, and an L, and this really is an O——"

20

" 'Tis Heslop," said old Jim. "It's his. Wheel me close, boy."

Young Jim brought the bath-chair alongside the tombstone. Old Jim leant forward with the tape-measure he had brought. He placed one end at the head of the tombstone and, with difficulty, stretched the length of it out. It was only a five-foot tape-measure, and it did not reach. Young Jim had to measure the remainder separately.

"Five feet," he said, "and another two feet nine inches."

"Nearly eight foot," said old Jim, and lay back in his chair and closed his eyes. "You must tell your sister that; you must tell them all that. Nearly eight feet his tombstone had to be, because in his life he was seven foot tall. There's his tombstone to prove it. Seven foot tall—they were giants in those days."

Then he opened his eyes again and said briskly: "What about the tea?"

Young Jim set the thermos flask and the biscuits out on the tombstone, as his grandfather told him. "He would never have minded," said old Jim, "any more than I should mind if you did it to me, when I'm gone. No, I should take it kindly."

They took turns at drinking out of the cup-top of the thermos flask, and ate digestive biscuits. The time was still not yet half-past six, but there was no doubt that the day was going to be another scorcher. The sun warmed them as they breakfasted, and old Jim spread his handkerchief over the top of his head for protection. Bees came out and began work among the tall weeds of the churchyard. A robin suddenly appeared at the far end of the tombstone, and young Jim threw him some biscuit crumbs.

Unexpectedly, a car passed: they just saw its roof over the top of the churchyard wall, and then—for a second—the whole of it as it passed the gap that was the churchyard gate. Then they heard brakes go on; the car seemed to stop abruptly, and then it backed until it was by the gate again, and then it stopped again. After a moment two policemen got out, and stared at them.

"Who's got a better right than we have?" said old Jim indignantly. "It's my grandfather's tombstone."

The policemen opened the churchyard gate and began walking up the path.

Old Jim and young Jim watched them.

The policemen left the main path and, in single file, came along the narrow path by the church, directly towards the Heslops.

When he was still some way away, the policeman in front called out, in an arresting voice: "James Heslop!" That he knew their name seemed ominous.

He did not go on at once—it was as if words failed him; but the second policeman burst out: "Whatever are you doing here, James Heslop, with your daughter-in-law and your mother off her head looking for you?"

The policemen now began to talk both at once.

"Running round the village looking for you," said the first policeman.

"In her dressing-gown," said the second policeman.

"Came to us in despair," said the first policeman.

"In her bedroom slippers," said the second policeman.

"And here we've been looking for you ever since," said the first policeman. "Now, what were you two up to?"

Both policemen waited for an answer to this. Neither old Jim nor young Jim said anything, so the second policeman said, "Eh?"

Old Jim smiled and shook his head, and young Jim cast his eyes down, putting himself out of the conversation altogether.

The second policeman said suddenly: "The old 'un's deaf—you remember she said so; and she said the child couldn't be got to talk much."

"Deaf?" said the first policeman. He drew a deep breath into his great chest, so that the blue bulk of it advanced until the silver buttons, moving from sunlight to sunlight, twinkled. With his breath very slowly going out, in a voice that might have wakened seven-foot James Heslop under his tombstone, the policeman shouted: "We've come to take you home in the car, Mr. Heslop." He added, with less voice—because he had less voice left: "The child can push the bath-chair back, empty." The policeman, when he had finished, looked tired and hollow-chested; old Jim smiled and shook his head.

"Deaf," said the second policeman.

Then the two policemen began to explain to old Jim, by gestures, what they intended. In dumb show they explained to him how they would help him into their car, and how comfortable he would be; they acted to him how swiftly and smoothly they would drive off—how soon they would get him safely home. Then they stopped to make sure he had understood. Old Jim clapped his hands and smiled; but he also shook his head.

The policemen started all over again, but, in the middle of their performance, one of them—perhaps losing patience—set his hands on the bath-chair as if to push it towards the car, with or without old Jim's permission. Then old Jim spoke, languidly—almost feebly: "I never like to be awkward, but I wouldn't like you to take on the responsibility of trying to get me into a car at my age. My joints are stiff, you know. And then there's my heart."

The policemen looked at old Jim carefully. He certainly appeared very frail, and he sounded very frail indeed. Yet they had promised Mrs. Heslop not only to find her father-in-law and her son, but to bring the old man home at once.

"Yet I'd like to be home, too," said old Jim. "It's been a strain—at my age—so early in the morning—so far. . . ." He let his voice die away, and closed his eyes.

"We should get him home somehow, quickly," said the first policeman, and the second nodded; they both looked anxious.

In the anxious silence, old Jim suddenly said, "Ah!" so that both policemen jumped. He had opened his eyes, and now he said: "You could tow me home."

"Tow you home?" repeated the policemen.

"Fasten my bath-chair to the back of your car with a tow-rope," said old Jim. "Pull me home on a tow-rope."

The policemen looked at each other, neither ever having been asked to tow anyone in a bath-chair before or heard of such a thing being done.

"It'd be a question for the Traffic Department, probably," said the first policeman.

"There'd be rules and regulations about it," said the second.

"For instance, he'd have to have his own number plate," said the first.

"Aye, he'd have been turned into a trailer."

Old Jim, not being able to follow the policemen's conversation, but seeing their hesitation, became impatient. "If you haven't a tow-rope, handcuffs would do. You could handcuff the bath-chair to the back of the car. Surely you have handcuffs in a police car."

"But you'd be a trailer!" shouted the first policeman.

"I'd be *what*?" asked old Jim—it was not clear whether he had not heard, or could not believe what he had heard.

The first policeman shook his head despairingly. "And it wouldn't be safe, anyway," he said.

"Unless, of course," said the second policeman, "we drove very slowly and carefully." He seemed to see possibilities in the idea after all.

"There is that," the first policeman agreed. "But however you look at it, he'd be a trailer: I doubt it wouldn't be legal."

At this point, young Jim surprised them by speaking. "But nobody'd see."

It was quite true: the hour was still so early that there was small danger of anybody's being on the roads between Little and Great Barley. On the other hand, the likelihood of such an encounter increased with every minute that the day advanced. If they were to act at all, they must act quickly.

The second policeman persuaded the first. It turned out, anyway, that they always carried a good rope in the boot. With this they fastened the front of the bath-chair—with old Jim still in it—to the back of the police car. Young Jim tucked his grandfather well into the chair, and then got into the back of the car. One policeman sat with him, and the other drove.

They went very slowly—that is, for a car, but much more quickly than a bath-chair could ever have been pushed. From the beginning to the end of the journey young Jim and the policeman with him kept watch through the rear window. Young Jim pressed his nose against the glass until it went white like a piece of pastry, and his eyes were very anxious.

At first old Jim looked anxious, too; but the faster he went the more confident he seemed to become. His white hair streamed in the wind, and he began to signal to the two at the back for the car to go faster still. They did not pass his message on to the driver. Already the bath-chair was travelling at a speed it had never dreamt of before: its whizzing wheels gave out an unbroken, high-

pitched squeak. "There'll be an accident!" the wheels screamed. "An accident!"

There was no accident; nor were they observed by anyone—unless you counted a horse looking over a gate beyond Little Barley. He watched their coming, but, when they were almost level with him, his nerve seemed to break, for he galloped off, with his back hooves wildly in the air. Old Jim waved to him with one hand, clinging to the side of the bath-chair with the other.

Not even in Great Barley were there people about, or traffic.

They turned into the housing-estate, and the only sign of life was a figure drooping over one of the front gates: Mrs. Heslop, waiting. The police car drew up beside her, and she looked at it, and at young Jim's face at the window, and at old Jim in the bath-chair behind. He was waving to her; and, now that the car engine was turned off, they could hear that he was singing—had probably been singing all the way. "Hearts of Oak" it must have been, because he now broke off at "Steady, boys, steady!"

Young Jim got out of the car quickly, and said: "Mum, I've come all the way from Little Barley in a police car!"

25

Mrs. Heslop shot out an arm—perhaps to catch him to her, perhaps to slap him; but instead of doing either she suddenly put both hands up to her face and burst into tears.

Poor Mrs. Heslop! Already it had been a long and very trying morning for her. She had not been woken at dawn by the gentle sounds of their setting forth; but a little later, waking of her own accord, she had listened to the silence of the house, and it had suddenly seemed to her unnatural in a way that it had never seemed before. She told herself that she was being foolish, and she tried to sleep again; but, in the end, she had got up and looked into young Jim's bedroom, and found him gone. Then she had found old Jim gone, and the bath-chair, too. Then she had started out wildly to look for them, and had only been sent home by the comforting promises of the police. Since then she had waited at the gate.

One policeman unhitched old Jim's bath-chair, while the other put his arm round Mrs. Heslop's shoulder and told her there was no need to cry now: everyone was safe and sound.

They all went indoors, and Mrs. Heslop recovered sufficiently to boil a kettle and make a pot of tea. The policemen stayed to drink a cup, and then went off; and then Mrs. Heslop settled down to cooking a proper, hot breakfast for old Jim and young Jim. "*Digestive biscuits!*" she snorted; and she served them with porridge and fried eggs and bacon and hot toast and marmalade, and more tea.

After breakfast, old Jim said that he was not really tired after all, and that he would like to sit out in the shade, in his usual chair, at the front of the house; and young Jim made him comfortable there. Young Jim wanted to stay with him, but Mrs. Heslop put her foot down and made him go upstairs to bed, where—sure enough—he was soon falling asleep.

Mrs. Heslop saw him into bed and drew his curtains against the bright sunlight, and left him: it was never much use, she knew, to question young Jim. She went downstairs and into the front garden. She planted herself in front of her father-in-law, so that he could not but pay some attention to her.

"Grandad!" she shouted. "Why did you *do* it?"

Old Jim nodded at her, and said: "And I hope they're having as good weather by the seaside. I've something to tell young Maisie, too, when she comes back. That reminds me——" He reached into his pocket and brought out the tape-measure. "Here's your tape-measure that we borrowed, my dear."

He held it out to Mrs. Heslop, and she took it, but as in a dream of amazement, and carelessly. She only held it by one end, so that the rest of the tape fell and rolled round her feet, encircling them.

Mrs. Heslop stared at the tape-measure and then at old Jim. "But why, Grandad—why—why——?"

"Aye," said the old man, "those days. . . ." He laughed to himself. "But what my grandfather would have said to see me bowling along this morning! The best of both worlds—that's what I've had."

"You and young Jim . . .," said Mrs. Heslop wonderingly, still standing within her magic circle of tape, staring at him. No longer was she expecting or hoping to be heard; but, oddly, this time old Jim must partly have heard her.

"Aye, he's a good boy." He blinked sleepily into the sunlight. "And, you know, although he's not big for his age, maybe he has the makings of a big man in him." His eyelids drooped, then rose again. "Maybe he'll grow to be six foot, after all, like his grandfather." Old Jim settled himself into his chair: he was going to sleep, and he knew it. "Or even seven foot, maybe, like his great-great-grandfather.' His eyelids fell again. He slept.

Upstairs in his bedroom, listening in his half-sleep to the booming voice from outside, young Jim had begun dreaming of giants and police cars.

27

Leon Garfield

Leon Garfield was born in 1921 in Brighton. For a while he was an art student, but after serving in Belgium and Germany during the Second World War he became a hospital biochemist. He began writing in his spare time but is now a full-time novelist. He lives in Highgate, London.

His first book for young readers, *Jack Holborn,* was published in 1964. As with most of his other work, including VAARLEM AND TRIPP, it is set in the eighteenth century; it is an exciting story about a young boy who becomes caught up with pirates. His second book, *Devil-in-the-Fog,* tells of the adventures of a boy who grows up with a family of travelling actors. His third, *Smith,* centres around a boy who witnesses a murder and is consequently pursued by the murderers. Other books include: *Mr Corbett's Ghost, Black Jack, The Restless Ghost* and *The Drummer Boy.*

His graphic descriptions of London and Southern England and his larger-than-life characters have caused him to be compared with Charles Dickens (see *SHORT STORIES THREE*), one of his favourite authors. He himself does not know what prompts him to write, "except that I feel restless when I don't". He explains his philosophy of writing thus:

"One does not write for children. One writes so that children can understand. Which means writing as clearly, vividly and truthfully as possible. Adults might put up with occasional lapses; children are far less tolerant. They must never be bored; not for an instant. Words must live for them; so must people. That is what really matters."

Vaarlem and Tripp

by Leon Garfield

It's certain he has a great gift: but otherwise he is a very contemptible, vile little man—strong-smelling, even, and well known in the Amsterdam courts for fraud, embezzlement and bankruptcy. It's very humiliating to be his pupil, but, as my father says, if God has planted a lily in a cess-pit, one must stop up one's nose and go down. Of late, my task has been to choose his brushes, pigment and canvas. He tells me this is as important a part of the craft of painting as there is, but the truth of the matter is that he's so much in debt and disgrace that he daren't show his face outside the studio. My name is Roger Vaarlem; my master is Joseph Tripp, of course.

A month ago he was before the Burghers who told him his portrait of the Admiral was unacceptable—insulting, even—and demanded their advance of guilders back. Having spent it, he offered to paint the Admiral again, but was not trusted: and rightly. Truth to Nature was one thing (no one could deny the portrait had a deal of truth in it, for my master has his gift), but truth to one's country and employers must come first. So he was given the opportunity of redeeming himself by painting a grand battle-piece to be hung in the Town Hall. Or prosecution in the courts again. Angrily (he told me) he accepted, and was granted a cabin aboard the *Little Willelm*. We sailed at half past eight this morning.

Though the early morning had been warm and brilliant, he was muffled in every garment he could find, careless of their cleanliness, which is a strong point aboard Dutch ships. It was very shameful to be walking along beside him, carrying his sketchbooks and other belongings which smelled worse than the tar and pickled fish with which the air was strong. There were two ships of ninety guns nodding in a stately fashion upon the gentle tide: cathedrals of gilded wood with triple spires and delicate crosses, netted and festooned like for a Saint's Day. The thought crossed my mind of parting from Mynheer Tripp and going to sea on my own, but my father would have prosecuted him for negligence and fraud and he'd have gone to gaol for it.

Then we came to the *Little Willelm* and he at once began to complain that it was insufficiently armed and pointed out the maze of stitching on the fore-topsail where English musket-fire had peppered it to a sieve. Together with all his other qualities, he is a great coward and I felt myself blush as he ranted on in the hearing of one of the ship's officers. Then, with my hand to his elbow, he went aboard, stepping down on the deck as if it were a single floating plank and not secure.

The *Little Willelm*, being but a smallish barquentine, could offer only a tiny cabin next to the surgeon's; but at least it was clean which flattered Mynheer Tripp unwarrantably.

"Go away, Vaarlem!" he mumbled, and crawled on to the bunk—for the motion of the ship at its moorings was already unsettling his stomach. So I left him and went out on to the maindeck in the sunny air and watched the crew go about their business in the rigging and on the yards.

"How come a fine-looking lad like you goes about with an old rag-bag like him?"

Mynheer Leyden—an officer of good family—was standing by me.

I answered: "Sir—he's a great man, whatever you may think, and will be remembered long after you and me are forgot."

After all, one has one's pride!

Mynheer Leyden would have answered, but Captain Kuyper began shouting from the quarter-deck to cast off and Mynheer Leyden shrugged his smooth shoulders and went about his duties. These seemed to consist in putting his hands behind his back and pacing the larboard rail, nodding to the crowd of fishwives and early clerks who always throng the harbour in the mornings to watch the glorious ships heave and puff out their sails like proud white chests and lean their way into the dangerous sea.

Once out of the harbour, the foresail was set and I went below to inform Mynheer Tripp he was missing a very wonderful sight, for there was not much wind and the great spread of canvas seemed to be but breathing against invisible, creaking stays. But he was already up and about—and in a more cheerful mood. He'd had intelligence that the *Little Willelm* was to sail west by south-west to lure enemy vessels into pursuit, when they'd be blown out of the water by our own great ships which would be following on the next tide. His cheerfulness arose from the discovery that the *Little Willelm* was the swiftest vessel in the Channel and was not intended to fight.

"A clean pair of heels, eh? Ha-ha!" he kept saying . . . and grinning in a very unwholesome manner. It was the only time I'd ever known him take a real pleasure in cleanliness. Later on, his spirits rose high enough for him to behave in his usual way. He began soliciting guilders from the officers to portray them prominently in the battle-piece. Full of shame—for he was earning a good deal of contempt—I warned him he'd be prosecuted for false pretences.

"Why?" he muttered angrily—the wind catching the soft brim of his black hat and smacking his face with it.

"Because they won't be larger than thumb-nails, sir!"

"You mind your own business, Vaarlem!" he snarled, quite beside himself where guilders were concerned. "If those little tinsel nobodies tell their dough-faced relatives that such and such blob of paint is their darling—well? Why not? What's wrong with a little family pride? Immortal, that's what they'll be! So keep your middle-class nose out of my affairs, Master Vaarlem . . . or I'll paint you as an Englishman!"

He stalked away, holding his hat with one hand and his filthy shawls and oil-stained coat with the other. But soon after, he sidled back again and remarked ingratiatingly, "No need to tell your papa everything I say, Roger, dear lad . . . words spoke in haste . . . no need for misunderstandings, eh? Dear boy . . ."

He was so mean, he was frightened my father would withdraw me as his pupil—and with me would go guilders. I looked at him coldly, while he bit his lip and brooded uneasily on whether he'd cut off his nose to spite his face; not that either would have been the loser.

I was more offended than I cared to let him know, so I obliged by keeping my nose out of his affairs for the remainder of the day. Which wasn't difficult, as he kept to the great cabin with the surgeon. Not that he was really ill—God forbid!—but he was cunningly picking the surgeon's wits relative to every ache and pain that plagued him. While all the while, the simple surgeon was happily imagining himself in the forefront of the Town Hall's battle-piece, a hero for ever. (Mynheer Tripp did indeed make a small sketch of him: a very wonderful piece of work—for somehow he caught a look of bewilderment and embarrassment in the surgeon's eyes as if God had too often stared them out.)

I'd intended to leave him for much longer than I did; at one time in the day I'd very serious thoughts indeed of leaving him altogether and fighting for Holland. This was when we saw our first English sail and there was great activity on the lower gun-deck against the chance of an encounter. She was a handsome, warlike vessel, bosoming strongly along. "A seventy-four," remarked Mynheer Leyden briskly. "By tomorrow she'll be drift-wood!" Then we outpaced her and the sea was as clean as a German silver tray.

It was a few minutes before half past eight o'clock in the evening. I'd been on deck together with several officers. The wind was gone. The air was still. A sharp-edged quarter moon seemed to have sliced the clouds into strips, so that they fell away slowly, leaving dark threads behind. Earlier, Mynheer Leyden had been urging me to speak with the captain relative to my becoming a midshipman, for I was of good family and too good for Mynheer Tripp. To be a painter was a lower-class ambition. ("All right! He has his gift! But what's that to you and me? God gave him sharp eyes—but He gave us good families! Vaarlem, my boy—I can't make you out!") Then, a few minutes before half past eight, he said quietly, "Vaarlem: you'd best go down and fetch him." Which I did.

"Sir: you must come up on deck at once."

Mynheer Tripp glanced at me irritably, began to mumble something, then thought better of it. He stood up and wrapped

32

himself in the filthy shawls and coat he'd strewn about the cabin.

"Hurry, sir!"

"Why? The sea won't run away . . . and if it does, I shan't be sorry!" He followed me on to the deck.

"Look, Mynheer Tripp! The Englishman!"

For a proud moment, I thought he'd had enough brandy to make him behave like a Dutchman, for he stood quite still and silent. Then the brandy's effect wore off and his own miserable spirit shone through. Every scrap of colour went from his face and he began to tremble with terror and rage!

"Madmen!" he shrieked—and I wished myself at the bottom of the sea and Mynheer Tripp with me. The Englishman was within half a kilometre, and still moving softly towards us, pulled by two longboats whose oars pricked little silver buds in the moonswept sea. She was as silent as the grave, and any moment now would turn, broadside on, and greet us with the roar of thirty-seven iron mouths. For she was the seventy-four.

Mynheer Tripp seized my arm and began dragging me towards the quarter-deck, shouting outrageously: "Move off! For God's sake move off! We'll all be killed! How dare you do such a thing! Look! Look! This boy . . . of a good family . . . very important! If he's harmed I'll be prosecuted by his father. And so will you! I demand to go back! For Vaarlem's sake! Oh, my God! A battle!"

They must have heard him aboard the Englishman. I could only pray that no one aboard it knew Dutch! I felt myself go as red as a poppy. To be used by this villainous coward as a mean excuse—I all but fought with him!

"You pig, Mynheer Tripp!" I panted. "This time you've gone too far!"

"Pig?" he hissed, between roarings at the captain. "You shut your middle-class mouth, Master Vaarlem! These noodles have no right to expose me—us to such danger! I'll sue—that's what I'll do! In the courts!"

Captain Kuyper—a man who'd faced death a hundred times and now faced it for maybe the last—stared at Mynheer Tripp as if from a great distance.

"You are perfectly right, sir. This ship is no place for you. You will be put off in the boat and rowed to where you may observe the engagement in safety. Or go to Holland. Or go to Hell, sir! As for the boy—he may stay if he chooses. I would not be ashamed to die in *his* company."

To my astonishment, before I could answer—and God knows what I'd have said—Mynheer Tripp burst out with: "How dare you, sir, put such ideas into a boy's head! What d'you expect him to say? A boy of good family like him! Unfair, sir! Cruel! Dishonest! What can he know? I warn you, if you don't put him off, I'll not stir from your miserable ship! Both of us—or none! Oh, there'll be trouble! In the courts!"

Then he turned his mean, inflamed face towards me and muttered urgently: "Keep quiet, Vaarlem! None of your business! Don't you dare say a word! I forbid it!"

Captain Kuyper shrugged his shoulders and turned away. "Put them both in the boat, and let one man go with them to take the oars. Immediately! I want Mynheer Tripp off this ship at once. Or by God, I'll throw him off!"

Quite sick with shame, I followed Mynheer Tripp, who'd scuttled to the boat and hopped into it, clutching his sketchbooks and horrible clothes about him—in a panic that the captain would do him a mischief.

The sailor who rowed us was a tall, silent fellow by the name of Krebs. For about twenty minutes he said nothing but rowed with a seemingly slow, but steady stroke. Mynheer Tripp, his head hunched into his shoulders, grasped my wrist and stared at the diminishing bulk of the *Little Willelm* which lay between us and the huge Englishman. Implacably, the Englishman came nearer and nearer and still did not turn. We could no more see the longboats . . . but the men in them must have had nerves of iron, for they were within musket range of the *Little Willelm* and could have been shot to pieces.

"Faster! Faster!" urged my master, as the bowsprit of the Englishman appeared to nod above the *Willelm*'s deck. There looked to be no more than fifty metres between them. Then she began to slew round . . . ponderously . . . malignantly. . . .

"Will you watch from here, sirs?" Krebs had stopped rowing. There was nothing contemptuous in the way he spoke. He simply wanted to know.

"Is it—is it safe?"

Krebs eyed the distance. "Most likely—yes, sir."

The two ships now lay side by side—the Englishman's aft projecting beyond the *Willelm*. Her after-castle, much gilded and gleaming under three lanterns, rose nearly as high as the *Willelm*'s mizen yard. A very unequal encounter. Perhaps she thought so? And was waiting for a surrender?

Krebs shipped his oars and stuck his chin in his great hands. Calmly he stared at the dark shape of his own ship, outlined against the sombre, spiky brown of her enemy. Though the shrouds and yards must have been alive with marksmen, nothing stirred to betray them.

"Thank God we ain't aboard!" he remarked at length. Mynheer Tripp nodded vigorously. He'd begun to make sketches by the light of a small lantern. Approvingly, Krebs glanced at them. Very workmanlike. I began to feel cold and lonely. Was I the only one who wished himself back aboard the *Little Willelm*?

The beginnings of a breeze. The great ghostly sails of the Englishman began to shift, but not quite to fill. The *Willelm*'s sails being smaller, bellied out more fatly. The bold little Dutchman and the skinny Englishman began to move. Masts, which had seemed all of one ship, began to divide—to part asunder. . . .

There seemed to be a moment of extraordinary stillness—even breathlessness—when suddenly a huge yellow flower of fire grew out of the side of the Englishman. (Beautiful Dutch lady—take my murdering bouquet!)

And then enormous billows of reddish smoke roared and blossomed up, blundering through the rigging and fouling the sails and sky. The engagement was begun.

A faint sound of screaming and shouting reached us, but was instantly drowned in the roar of the *Willelm*'s broadside. Then the Englishman fired again—this time with grapeshot, which makes an amazing, shrieking sound as it flies.

"The mainmast! D'you see? They've got the mainmast!" muttered Krebs, his face white even in the reddish glare of the encounter. "Shrouds and halyards cut through—murder for them on deck! Slices them in two and three parts! Murder, it is!"

The *Willelm* was still firing—but not full broadsides. Half her ports must have been shattered.

"They've got to heave the dead out of the way!" Krebs said very urgently—as if it was his immediate task. "Can't get to the powder quick enough with all them dead tangling up the trunnions . . . got to heave 'em out . . . Cap'n'll be down there now—he'll be doing the right thing—"

Another flash and roar from the Englishman: not so vast as the first. Was she disabled, too?

"Quarter-deck cannon," mumbled Krebs, suddenly scowling. "Now you'll see—" Again, she roared. "Upper deck cannon . . . fourteen killers there!" A third blaze and roar. Krebs nodded. "Lower deck. They know what they're at. Give no chance . . . no chance at all. . . ."

The *Willelm* seemed to have stopped firing. "Look! Poor devils up in the cross-trees. D'ye see? Firebrands! Nought else left! But they'll never reach to the Englishman. Poor devils! Oh, God! She's

afire herself! Keep your heads down, sirs! She'll be going up in a minute! A-ah!"

Even as he spoke, the fire must have reached the *Willelm*'s powder store. There was a glare and a thunderous crackling sound like the end of the world—as indeed for many it was. With a shriek of terror, Mynheer Tripp—who'd been extraordinarily absorbed throughout the encounter, oblivious to everything but his rapid, intent drawing—flung himself to the bottom of the boat: a quaking bundle of disgusting rags. Then the great light went out of the sky and the air was full of smoke and the sharp, bitter smell of spent powder and burnt out lives. Pieces of wood began to kiss the water about us. When at last the smoke drifted up to the moon, we saw the guilty hump of the Englishman sliding away, leaving nothing more behind than a torn-up patch of sea, rough with drift-wood and darknesses.

"Oh, God! Now what's to become of us?" wept Mynheer Tripp. I begged him to be quiet, for things were bad enough without his assistance. Krebs had been hit in the neck by a flying piece of iron and was bleeding like a pig. If he wasn't bandaged, he'd die. Mynheer Tripp plucked at one of his shawls—not offering it, but indicating that, if pressed, he'd part with it. It was filthy enough to have killed Krebs outright: by poisoning. There was nothing for it but to use my shirt; which I did, watched by Mynheer Tripp who snarled when I tore it into strips:

"I hope you know that was your best linen, Vaarlem!"

Which mean remark did nothing but gain me unnecessary thanks from Krebs who could scarcely speak: his wound having severed a tendon and opened a great vessel. He lay in the bottom of the boat while I took the oars, watched by that dirty jelly in the stern. All I could see of Mynheer Tripp were his miserably reproachful eyes.

"You'll die of cold," he mumbled furiously.

"*I* can keep warm by rowing, sir!" I said, hoping to shame him. I pulled towards the *Little Willelm*'s grave in the frail hope of survivors, but found none. Then, under Kreb's whispered directions, I began to row eastward, into the path of our hoped-for followers on the coming tide. But, being no craftsman of oars, we did little more than drift in that dark and hostile sea: Mynheer Tripp, Krebs and me. For two or even three hours. . . . As

Mynheer Tripp had predicted, it was violently cold. I began to shiver and sweat at the same time. My hands were growing very sore and swollen. When I paused to shift my grip, I found them to be bleeding; and Mynheer Tripp, without once stopping, moaned and cursed the sea and the murdering Englishman. Which served no purpose at all. But then he's not the best of companions in such circumstances. He hates the sea and can't abide the sight of blood. Also, there are a million other things capable of panicking him. The chief problem is to avoid being infected by this.

At about one o'clock the breeze began to blow more briskly and in a changed direction. Long bands of cloud began to shift and obscure the moon. The darkness grew thick and formidable; Mynheer Tripp's eyes were no longer visible—but I felt their continuing reproach. Krebs was quite silent and, every now and again, I thought he'd died and had to stop rowing to put my head to his chest and be greeted with: "Still here . . . don't you worry . . . keep it up, boy—" So back I'd go to my task, abysmally cold and frightened, but not wanting to give the odious Mynheer Tripp the opportunity for gloating.

Then I thought we were saved! Lanterns glinted high up in the night ahead. Our ships at last! I shouted and waved the dim remains of our lantern. Krebs struggled up on his elbow. He said, "It's the Englishman again!"

"Douse the light, Vaarlem!" shrieked Mynheer Tripp. But it was too late. We'd been seen. The Englishman hailed us.

"Ahoy, there!" Which, in Dutch, means, "Stand fast or we'll pepper you with musket fire!"

Nearer and nearer she came, a glinting, ghostly monster. Mynheer Tripp began to gabble we'd be tortured and hanged. I never felt more ashamed of him in my life. He was quaking with terror. I sweated to think of how the English would sneer . . . a craven Dutchman. Maybe I could swear he was French: or German? The great ship was alongside. The murderous cannon still poked out of their ports like blunt black teeth against the dark sky. Two English sailors came down on ropes and hoisted Krebs between them. I was surprised by how like Dutchmen they looked. We were bidden to follow, when Mynheer Tripp further disgraced our nation by being frightened of falling off the rope.

"For God's sake, sir!" I hissed at him. "Make a good showing."

"What d'you mean, 'for God's sake', Vaarlem?" he hissed back. "You nasty little prig!"

With much contemptuous laughter, more sailors came and helped Mynheer Tripp up between them. I followed on my own. No sooner was I on deck than Mynheer Tripp—who'd got a considerable, jeering crowd about him, shouted in his bad English: "Cover him up! Boy of good family, that! He'll die of cold!" I flushed angrily, but a huge cloth was brought and wrapped round me. To my indignation, I saw it was an English flag. I stripped it off and flung it down.

"I'd *rather* die of cold than be covered with that!" I meant to display *some* Dutch spirit and show we weren't all like Mynheer Tripp.

"Brave lad!" said an officer—the Captain, I think. "Worthier than his companion, eh? What say we heave the old fellow back?"

I grew alarmed. Begged them to do no such thing. "Though you may not think it, he's a great man . . . greater than all of us put together!"

"A greater coward, you mean, boy! How come you go about with such a rag-bag?"

But fortunately, Mynheer Tripp hadn't heard the threat. He was by the mizen-mast lantern, examining his drawings to see they were intact. A number of officers and sailors were staring over his shoulder. Then more and more came, with more lanterns, lighting up that patch of deck which seemed roofed with canvas and walled by the netted shrouds. Krebs and his honourable wound, and myself and my defiance were left and forgotten. A greater victory was in the making. Of a sudden, I began to feel very proud to be Mynheer Tripp's pupil, and my eyes kept filling with tears on that account. I picked up the flag and wrapped out the cold with it, and went to join the English crowd about my master. Krebs, feeling stronger, leaned on me and stared.

Not all the ships and cannon and defiance in the world could have done what he'd done. With a few lines—no more—he'd advanced into the enemies' hearts and set up his flag there. Mynheer Tripp's victory had been with God's gift—not with the gunsmith's. It's a mercy, I suppose, he never really knew his own

power—else he'd have suffocated it under guilders. The Englishmen stared at his drawings, then, seeing Krebs, began comparing with him—in slow English and bad Dutch—the terror and grandeur of their experience, so uncannily caught by the sniffing and shuffling Mynheer Tripp. Pennants, flags, even countries were forgotten. An aspect of battle was seen with neither Dutch nor English eyes, but with a passion and a pity that encompassed all.

"Mynheer Tripp," said the English Captain—a handsome, well-bred man, most likely of Dutch descent, "you are a very great man. We are honoured. As our guest, sir, I invite you to visit England."

My master looked at me—not with pride or any so respectable a thing, but with his usual greed and cunning. He said, in his horrible English, "Good! Good! I will paint your Admiral, maybe—?"

And then to me in Dutch, with an offensive smirk: "You see, Vaarlem, these English are different. I told you so. I'll be appreciated—not prosecuted. Just wait till they see what I make of *their* Admiral! Money back, indeed! And after all, my boy, guineas is as good as guilders, eh? He-he!"

He really is the most contemptible man I know! I wonder what the English will make of him: and what he'll make of the English?

41

William Mayne

William Mayne was born in 1928, the eldest of five children of a doctor and a nurse. He was educated at the Canterbury Cathedral Choir School, which provided the setting for his third novel, *A Swarm in May,* the book that established him as a leading author for young people. It tells the story of John Owen, the youngest chorister at the school, who refuses to carry on tradition by acting as the cathedral's beekeeper, thinking he dislikes bees. But in helping the organist with his swarm, he discovers quite the opposite and also makes other exciting discoveries among the cathedral towers. Subsequent Choir School novels are *Chorister's Cake, Cathedral Wednesday* and *Words and Music.*

Several of his other books are set in the Yorkshire Dales, where he spent his own childhood and where he worked for a time as a schoolteacher. He has also worked for the BBC, although he has mostly been a full-time writer. Altogether he has produced more than twenty books for children, including *A Grass Rope, Earthfasts* and *Ravensgill.* He has also edited a number of anthologies.

Most of his stories are for older children, who are better able to appreciate the clever way he evokes place and atmosphere, as in A HAUNTED TERRACE and A PRINCE IN THE BUILDING, and his brilliant characterisation, of which THE TEST is a particularly good example. This story first appeared, in fact, in an anthology for adult readers.

William Mayne lives in the village of Thornton Rust in his beloved Yorkshire. He does all his writing and a great deal of reading in his comfortable stone cottage overlooking the Fells.

A Haunted Terrace

by William Mayne

We live in a good house, but only at the top. There's one thing about a flat: you don't get noticed every time you go out of the front door, because you might be somebody from the other two flats, so I can slip in and say goodnight and then go out again. Roger didn't have to be in home until an hour after me, and then I would go in again very quiet, and be looking asleep when Mum came in to see about the window being open and that awful yellow convent dress being hung up, because it had to last a week, and wasn't made of drip-dry or non-crease, which wouldn't have cost more, but it would have been twice as useful. I ought to say about the house. It's the end one of a very long row, and right at the other end Jennifer lives. She's in the fourth form with me, and about thirty more, but they don't matter for now, though they do at school because of their way of knowing too much and getting above me. Of course, they haven't got Roger to fuss over, which I have when they're swotting, but Roger needs that much looking after, you wouldn't believe, though I only took him out of kindness when he had that purple on his face to cure his skin which he got from his sister, so he calls her his skin and blister, instead, rhyming, which is his way of talking. He comes from London, because his father's with the Admiralty down here, and he hasn't much to do with this I'm telling you, so I won't say anything about him. I'm not going really steady with him, he's only my second, and you don't want a steady until about your fourth.

Jennifer lives at the other end of the terrace, but it isn't a straight row. We don't go much for straight rows in Bath, not in the good

43

houses. Ours is good, and you see pictures of it on calendars, for beauty. It was built two hundred years ago by a man called Wood, but the rooms are quite big and high, not like cottages. The row goes in a curve, part of a circle, with sixty houses in it, and there aren't any opposite, only the Royal Terrace Gardens, because the houses are the Royal Terrace. I remember the builder's name, because it's ours, too, Wood.

That's the explanation of it, but I'll say what happened. I went in one night, just on nine, but a bit after, and Mum said "You're late, Margaret."

"Only just," I said. "I think I've left something downstairs," I really meant I wanted to go down and tell Roger I'd been caught, but Mum knew.

"He can stay down," she said. "And you can stay up."

I said, "If I can stay up, why can't I go out again?"

"I mean you can stay upstairs," said Mum. "Off to bed." She said she'd hung up that dress, too, which I wouldn't wear out in case Bonzo heard of me. She's the head of the convent and she wouldn't see me herself, but Mrs. White could have, unless I was in my jeans and my hair different. I pretended not to know her once, and she looked at me for lipstick the next day, but I'd got it off, so she thought she was wrong.

This night I went into my bedroom. It's at the front, and I looked out of the window, and Roger was there about an inch high on the road. Mum was still on the landing, so I leant out low to stop her hearing and talked to Roger. I thought the sound wouldn't get back up, because there's a ledge under the window, and I got my chin below it. Roger thought I would fall out, but I didn't. I talked to him for a bit, and he said "See you tomorrer, ugly horrer", which is what we say, and I said "After tea, bumble bee", which is what I say, but we made it up, and you aren't supposed to know it if you aren't us two. Then Mum began to come in, so I got in, and Roger went away because he's a bit shy of Mum, because he lives in a square prefab and our house is better, but I'd rather have a prefab and get out of the window.

In the morning I met that Jennifer, and she said "After tea, bumble bee", so I gave her one with my satchel, because she must have been listening in the Royal Terrace Gardens. She said she

hadn't, and blamed me off for talking under her window, so I gave her another for telling a lie, because she must have been in the Gardens. I think she was jealous because her Miles, or whatever his name was, was off with a Secondary Modern girl in Bathwick, and I don't blame him, but I don't know how she could be jealous of Roger, he isn't a treat, and such a bother to get tidy before I'll go with him.

But I had to think something different a day or two later. It wasn't dark when I went to bed, because of the summer, and I was just looking at the ceiling, when somebody said my name, like Samuel in the temple, which we did in non-Catholic R.I. You would think you were dreaming to hear that. I did, so I thought I would swallow my tongue and choke if I was lying on my back any more and going to sleep. You might. So I turned over and shut my eyes, and somebody said "Margaret" again, like the Forsaken Merman whose wife was called that, only she was human. So am I, of course, so I sat up and said "Mum, did you call me?"

She said she hadn't, have you hung up that dress? Well, I did that, and put the light out again, and said the window was open and went to bed again, but it wasn't any use, because somebody said "Margaret" again.

It wasn't Roger, unless his voice had unbroken again. It was very broken just then, and he could sing in two voices if he liked, if you could call it singing. He could do it separately or together, but he couldn't talk except deep, with squeaks.

Anyway, I got the idea it came from the window, so I went to it and listened, without looking out, and whoever it was said it again. It sounded as if it came from just outside in the air, but nobody was there, of course. So I looked out, and the voice said "Hello."

Nobody was there, even in the Gardens, but I couldn't be certain, they might have been, but the voice didn't sound as if it came from down below at all, it was just by me. I shut the window down and bolted it and drew the curtains and got well into bed, and got as hot as butter and just as sticky. I didn't like it.

Next day I asked Roger if he'd done it, but he said no, cross his horse and cart, which is heart, and slit his pearly, which he says is London for throat, only he says froat. I kept that window closed for another night, but it was too hot the next, and I thought I might have been dreaming, and then I thought of Joan of Arc, and you never know, it might be like Samuel. So I thought I ought to listen, in case, except if they wanted me to be a nun I wouldn't because I can't wear black, except the jeans.

Well, it came again, and I got to the window at once. There was nothing to see at all, only the gasworks the other side of the Gardens, and even that wasn't easy to see because of the sun setting behind it. It shone all into the terrace. It shone in my room last of all, which made it hottest of them. The voice came whispering out again. I thought it might be someone in the next window, but it wasn't. It said "Margaret" again, and then it said "I am going to haunt you."

"You'd better not," I said, because I didn't want it to.

"I shall," it said, "my little bumble bee."

There was nobody in sight at all. Not even anyone walking about anywhere. At least there was one person, and I noticed her by her colour. It was Jennifer, hanging out of her window, but her house is the other end of the Terrace, and she was up near the sunset. I knew her by her hair, which is the red sort people are proud of, and don't let you call red, but urban, or something, like the city council dust carts, but not in colour because they are green.

I put the window down again and sweated to death under the blankets again. I would rather do that than be haunted.

The next night I thought there must be somebody, so I put Roger in the Gardens when I came in. Mum was pleased to see me so early, but I didn't get undressed, I only waited, after I'd put the light out. It sort of needs a light to go to bed by, even if it isn't dark. I told Roger to look out for people, and when the voice came again, just saying "Margaret", I waved to him, and he began to look. But there was no one there.

I leaned out quickly, and told him to look everywhere. But he didn't see anyone; and before I had waved goodbye to him the voice said "There is no one to be seen. I am a ghost, little bumble bee."

Jennifer was looking out of her window again, so I didn't want to look a fool standing at the window watching the sunset, so I sat inside, still dressed, because clothes make you braver.

The voice said "I will haunt you, Margaret", and then it said "Ow", as if it had got hit, and stopped. So I went to bed with the window open. It didn't say any more that night.

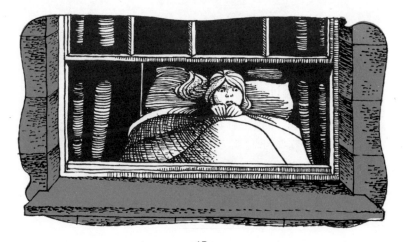

47

The next day Jennifer wasn't at school I noticed, because I was going to ask her whether she had heard the voice, too. She might have been at her window listening like me. I thought I might go round after her and see whether she had. She might have been haunted ill, I thought, seeing she wasn't there, and I thought it might happen to me.

At dinnertime somebody bought a paper, and they brought it to me and showed me a bit, and there was the voice, printed down, mysterious haunting of Royal Terrace by disembodied voice, saying what the voice said, about "I will haunt you, little bumble bee". So I wasn't the only one, and I didn't mind it any more.

I showed it to Roger, and he didn't know what disembodied meant either. He doesn't know a thing. He'd been tattooing himself with Quink, and he looked as if he had the purple skin stuff on again. When he had gone I listened again, and the voice came; but this time, all along the Terrace, people looked out, which I thought was odd, to have such a long voice. It hadn't said more than "Margaret" once, when there was a great noise, like a crowd talking, and they began to say "It's that girl at the end", and the people began to leave the windows and come down into the road; so I got the door open and went down, too.

The people were all going to the other end, so I went, too. They went right along, and looked up, and there was Jennifer, with that hair hung out of the window, talking to herself, saying "Margaret, I will haunt you, my little bumble bee", until someone in the crowd of us said, "Hey, can't you be quiet, we can hear you all along the row."

Jennifer heard that, and hopped in at once, and put the window down. Mr. Mortimer, who lives in the middle, with a whole house to himself, went up to their flat and in a little while he came down and stood on the steps with his hand up for silence, and he told us how voices went round curved buildings, like the Whispering Gallery in St. Paul's in London, and it wasn't a haunting but a foolish schoolgirl talking to her friend at the other end of the Terrace. They meant me, at the other end, but I'm not a friend of Jennifer.

I told her next day she was a foolish schoolgirl, but she was still puffed up at having found out about voices going along curves, because she had heard me talk to Roger that way, which was how she knew about the bumble bee. I asked Roger about Whispering Galleries in St. Paul's, but he said he had never been up there because there were too many apples and pears, which is London for stairs. He's no use at knowing anything.

49

John Rowe Townsend

John Rowe Townsend was born in 1922 in Leeds. For twenty years he was an editor with a national newspaper and his first book, published in 1961, arose partly from his work as a journalist.

"I had come to the conclusion .. that children's books were too harmless, hygienic and middle-class .. too little engaged with things that mattered. I'd been writing some articles that involved going round on the beat with the NSPCC (National Society for the Prevention of Cruelty to Children) inspectors, and I felt that children should be able to read about this other side of childhood." This view coincided with another interest he had at that time. "I had a visual obsession with a certain industrial district where a tangle of grimy streets sloped down to a canal bank .. I started wandering round it, putting imaginary people into it." Eventually he began writing *Gumble's Yard*.

It is a story about a family of children in a very poor slum home. The couple who are supposed to be looking after them walk out and the children set up house on their own in a deserted warehouse by a canal bank. When it first appeared, it was thought by many people to be too sordid for children but it soon became very popular. Since then, John Rowe Townsend has written many other books including *Hell's Edge, Widdershins Crescent* (a follow-up to *Gumble's Yard*) and *The Intruder* (which won an award from the Mystery Writers of America).

As you will see from THE FRIDAY MIRACLE, he aims to make the characters and situations he creates as real as possible. He also believes that "the first class book for children is never grown out of".

The Friday Miracle

by John Rowe Townsend

At twenty past three the mothers started arriving at the school. The school was a private one. It was a big old house in a wide street in a pleasant, gently decaying part of the city.

The mothers arrived in their Minis and Vivas and little Fiats. They got out of their cars and stood around on the pavement, chatting till the children appeared. Willis didn't chat with the mothers. Willis was aloof. Willis drew up at the other side of the street and sat in the Daimler, motionless.

At half past three school ended and out came the children. Some of the smallest ran straight to their mothers' arms. Some sauntered out in twos and threes, joking and laughing. Some fought and shouted and whizzed round in circles, letting off steam.

Ronald and Avril and Ben always walked out sedately, side by side. They looked both ways and crossed the road to Willis and got in the car. Avril thought Willis ought to open the door for them, but he didn't, except on Fridays.

Ben was only seven, and sometimes he boasted at school about Willis and the Daimler.

"We have a chauffeur and a big grey Daimler and another big car at home," he'd say, "and my father has a Jaguar, and once he came to meet us in it."

But the children in his class didn't care.

"My father drives a car transporter," Simon Malory had answered once, but everyone knew that wasn't true.

Ronald and Avril didn't boast. They were twelve and ten, and they were quiet. They had friends at school but they didn't see

them outside, because friendships out of school seemed to start with chats between mothers on the pavement, and arrangements for lifts, and casual invitations to tea. Friendships out of school didn't go with Willis and the Daimler.

Ronald and Avril walked quietly each day to the car with Ben between them. They held one of Ben's hands each, to keep him safe and in order. They walked out of school as they walked into school—not really looking forward to the hours ahead, but ready to put up with them because putting up with them was all you could do.

Except on Fridays, and today was Friday.

On Fridays they ran across the road (just remembering to look both ways and to keep hold of Ben's hands). On Fridays Barbara came and sometimes Father, and Willis opened the door for them. Friday was the day they went to Granny Taylor's. There was no day like Friday.

Today they tumbled into the car, and Willis shut the door and went round to the driver's seat and the car drew away from the kerb. Willis didn't say a word. Willis knew the routine.

It was a pity, thought Ronald and Avril, that Father wasn't there. But Father didn't often come these days. They'd almost given up expecting him.

Ben was excited, as he always was on Fridays.

"Will Heinz Dog be there?" he asked. "Will the Thorpes be at home? Can Stan and Alice help me make a den in the back yard? What will we have for tea?"

"How should I know, Ben?" Barbara said. Barbara was Father's second wife.

"How should Barbara know?" said Avril, echoing her. "We don't know till we get there, do we?"

It took twenty minutes to get to Granny Taylor's. Granny Taylor's was a fair-sized, solid red-brick terrace house, one of six. It had a lion knocker on the front door, and if Granny wasn't there to meet them in the doorway Ben always rushed to the knocker and beat a great rat-tat on it.

Today Ben rat-tatted but Granny Taylor didn't come as quickly as usual. Ronald and Avril stood behind Ben. Willis didn't wait. Willis handed two or three parcels out and said "Six-thirty then, ma'am," and in a moment the Daimler was gone.

Ben rat-tatted again.

"That's funny," Barbara said. "She knows we always come on Fridays."

Then at last Granny Taylor opened the door, and there were great huggings and kissings, and it wasn't until they were all in the house that they saw that she was limping.

"Whatever have you been doing?" Barbara asked.

"I fell," said Granny Taylor. She looked guilty.

"You *naughty* old thing," Barbara said.

"I couldn't help it. It was that dark corner on the cellar stairs. I slipped."

"And I'm not surprised," said Barbara. She sounded just as if she was talking to Ben. "At your age you shouldn't set foot on those cellar stairs. Now let me look. You've got a bandage under that stocking, haven't you? . . . Ronald and Avril, you can go outside for a few minutes while I talk to your Granny."

Ben had gone already. He'd disappeared through the back door in search of Stan and Alice Thorpe and their dog Heinz. Ronald and Avril followed as far as the yard. Barbara's voice came down to them from the kitchen window.

"It seems to be going on all right," she was saying, "but it's a wonder it wasn't worse. You might have broken your leg, if not your neck. I can't trust you, darling, can I?"

Ronald pulled a face at Avril.

"Poor old Gran," he said. "She's in trouble today."

Then he pushed open the gate into the next yard. Avril knew he'd be looking for Tom Sutton next door. Tom's father had a workshop and tools, and he didn't mind if Tom and his friends used them. Ronald could never wait to get his hands on those tools.

Avril stayed where she was. She heard Barbara's voice again from the kitchen window. And this time came the shock.

"I'm not going to let you stay here *any* longer," Barbara was saying to Granny Taylor. "This time I mean it. I shall tell Jim, it's absolutely *impossible* for you to stay here."

"But I've lived here forty years, dear," Granny Taylor said. "It's my home."

"Forty years! All the more reason for leaving. It's so old-

54

fashioned and awkward. It's too much for you, you know it is. *And* it's so shabby."

"Well, it's big enough, that's true," said Granny Taylor. "There's room for all of you here, if you wanted to come."

Avril moved away from the window because she could hear every word and it felt as if she was eavesdropping. But she couldn't get what had been said out of her mind.

She pushed open the door into the next yard. Ronald was there with Tom Sutton, and they didn't notice her because they were busy making some mysterious object with Tom's father's drill, and all round them were hammers and screwdrivers and planes and pieces of wood and shavings. From two or three doors farther on she could hear the barking of Heinz and the shouts of Ben, playing with Stan and Alice Thorpe. "There's room for all of you here, if you wanted to come." If they lived there it would be like a week of Fridays. But it looked more as if Granny Taylor would be leaving than as if they'd be coming here.

Avril wandered back into the house and helped to lay the kitchen table. They were going to have tea. Scrambled eggs on toast and brown bread and butter and jam and fruit salad and chocolate biscuits and cake.

"I can't think how these children ever get up from the table, with the food you give them," Barbara said to Granny Taylor. "And they're supposed to have their supper at seven. It throws everything out when they come here."

"I'm sorry, dear," Granny Taylor said. Barbara returned to the first subject.

"And this accident happened at the weekend," she said, "and you never told us. You could have let us know, couldn't you? After all, Jim is your only son, and the children *are* your only grandchildren, and you should *tell* us when a thing like this happens."

"Jim's so busy," Granny Taylor said.

"Well, yes, he is busy. A business the size of his, and growing all the time. He gets so tired and worried. There's some kind of special meeting going on now that's worrying him. But he does think about you, you know."

"I haven't seen him since Easter."

55

"He thinks about you a lot. He says he'll come as soon as the present problems are sorted out."

"There's always something to be done before I see him," said Granny Taylor.

"There's nothing to stop you coming to see us any time," Barbara said. "You know I'll always send Willis round for you."

"I don't like it in that cold house," Granny Taylor said.

"It's not a cold house. It has full central heating."

"Well, it feels cold to me."

"You're an obstinate old woman," said Barbara. She patted Granny's arm, as if to say she wasn't really cross. But she did sound cross all the same . "You're not fit to be on your own."

Granny Taylor turned off the gas and ladled scrambled eggs on to plates.

"Go and call the others," she said to Avril.

Avril went for the others. Ben broke away at once from what he was doing, ran into the house and sat at the table, waiting. He loved his meals. Ronald didn't come so quickly. He and Tom Sutton had reached a vital stage of their work. But he came soon enough. Barbara was the only person who didn't much care for high tea at Granny Taylor's. She sipped a cup of tea and ate a biscuit.

Afterwards the boys let Avril help them for a while—mostly holding things—and then she joined Ben and the Thorpes, who'd made a house with blankets and a couple of clothes-horses. Then Susan Gough at the end house came out, and she and Avril knocked a tennis-ball about between them. Then it was half past six and they were brushing themselves down and Willis was waiting with the car. Granny Taylor sighed a little as she kissed them good-bye.

"Well," said Barbara to Avril as one woman to another, when they were sitting together in the back seat, "this time she's learned her lesson. I gave her a good talking-to. She realizes now, she'll just have to give the house up."

"What, Granny leave her home?"

"She's getting to an age when she just can't cope," Barbara said.

Ronald leaned over.

"Where will she go?" he asked. "Will she come and stay with us?"

"No, she wouldn't want to. But we can get her into Sunsets. It's very nice there. It's a kind of hotel for elderly people where they get properly looked after. It almost makes me wish I was old. They have rooms of their own, with all their possessions round them. It's expensive, of course, but your father doesn't mind paying. It will be a relief to us to know she's under supervision."

"But she won't like it," said Ronald slowly.

"Oh yes, she will when she's used to it. She'll be very happy there."

"I shan't like it," said Avril. "I shan't like it at all."

Ben had been listening. Suddenly he burst into tears.

"I won't see Heinz Dog any more," he wailed. "Or Stan or Alice. We won't be able to play in our den."

"You don't want a silly old den of blankets," said Barbara. "And as for that mongrel, well, I bear it no malice but it really is a revolting creature . . ."

"I love him," said Ben. "I love Heinz Dog. And Stan and Alice." He sobbed and sobbed. "I don't want to stop going to Granny Taylor's house."

"Nor do I," said Ronald.

"No more lovely Fridays," said Avril. There was a lump in her throat.

"Now don't be silly," Barbara said. "You'll still be able to see Granny Taylor. And probably still on Fridays, if that's what you want."

"But it won't be the same," said Avril.

"No, it won't," said Ronald, fiercely. "Not at all."

"It'll just be school and home and Father always busy and never anything nice," said Avril.

Ben burst into fresh wailings. Ronald and Avril bit their lips.

"Oh, my goodness," said Barbara. "What next? It isn't the end of the world."

"It is," said Avril. She took Ben's and Ronald's hands. "I wish a miracle would happen," she said. "A Friday miracle. If there's a day for miracles, I'm sure it's Friday."

But it didn't look the time or place for a miracle. Willis drove

57

steadily on, his back stiff and unyielding. Willis didn't know and didn't care what happened in the back of the car. Willis did his job.

The children weren't taking notice of anything when the car turned into their own drive. But Barbara sat up straight and spoke in surprise.

"They're still all there!" she said.

"Who are?"

"The people who came for the special meeting I was telling you about."

There were half a dozen cars, all biggish, some chauffeur-driven, parked in the drive. Willis slid past them in the Daimler, stopped at the portico, opened the car doors for Barbara and the children, then drove off towards the garage.

Ben's face was still tearful. Barbara bent down and dabbed at it with the corner of her handkerchief.

"Can't have you going in to see your father like that," she said.

Then the front door opened and the gentlemen who owned the cars came out. They were middle-aged or elderly, well-dressed, solemn. They didn't seem to want to talk. They raised their hats, passed the time of day briefly, and went on to their cars. One of them noticed Ben's tear-stained face, looked at Barbara with sympathy, and said,

"I'm very sorry, Mrs. Taylor. No wish of mine that this should happen." And he followed the others.

Then Father was at the door. He was smiling. He came out and caught them all in his arms—all at once in a bunch.

"Well!" he said. "It's all over. Finished. Problems solved at one fell swoop." He released them.

Barbara looked out between the pillars across the acre-and-a-half of lawn to where the last car was just disappearing through the big wrought-iron gates.

"Jim, please explain," she said.

"We had a business," Father said. "Now we haven't. Tomorrow I'll be furious at the thought of ten years' wasted work. But today at this moment I just feel free."

"You mean they've bought you out?" Barbara said.

"Not exactly. International Castings have taken the business over, debts and all. Which is just as well, seeing there's more debts

58

than anything else. We tried to expand too fast and ran into trouble. They know about the debts, of course, but they still want to get their hands on the firm."

"So you haven't a job," Barbara said.

"Not just now. But I'm a trained engineer. I'll get a job soon."

"And you haven't any money?"

"Not a cent."

"And the cars?"

"They're the firm's cars. They go with the business."

"And how will we keep this house up?"

"We won't," Father said. "Henry Morris of International says he'll take it over, staff and all. He's had his eye on it for years. So you see. No job, no money, no car, no home. No problems."

"Except where we're going to live," said Barbara.

Ben's voice piped up.

"Granny Taylor has a house," he said, "she says there's room for all of us there."

"Don't be silly, Ben," said Barbara, and then, "You'll have to give me time, Jim. I can't get used to all this in five minutes."

"Ben's idea's not so silly as all that," Father said. "We could stay there a little while, perhaps, if she'd have us."

"We could look after her," Avril said.

"We could change schools," Ronald said, "and not pay any money any more."

"'Course she'll have us," said Ben. "'Course she'll have us. Let's go and tell her right away."

"What we need first is some dinner," said Father. He thought for a moment and said, "Well, why shouldn't we go across and see your Granny?" Then he added, "On the bus, of course."

Ben loved buses. He jumped up and danced with delight, all by himself. And as he danced he sang,

"We're off to Granny Taylor's on the bus. We're off to Granny Taylor's on the bus."

Ronald and Avril, Father and Barbara watched him. They all knew life wasn't as simple as it seemed to Ben. They didn't know what would happen to them. But they smiled, all of them smiled.

Rudyard Kipling

Rudyard Kipling was born in 1865 in Bombay. From 1871 to 1877 he was brought up by a Mrs. Holloway in Southsea, England, while his parents remained in India. They were the most unhappy years of his life: Mrs. Holloway was a strict, over-religious woman and her son was a merciless bully. The next five years were spent at a school in Devon, after which Kipling went back to India where he became a journalist. When he returned to London in 1894 he had had a number of books published but had yet to write his most famous stories.

The first of these, *The Jungle Book,* appeared shortly after his return, followed a year later by *The Second Jungle Book*. These collections of stories are perhaps best remembered for the tales about Mowgli, a boy who is raised by a family of wolves and grows up with the wild animals of the Indian jungle. However, some of the non-Mowgli tales, such as the one about RIKKI-TIKKI-TAVI the mongoose, are also well known.

Other books which have been enjoyed for many years by both children and adults are: *Kim,* about a thirteen-year-old boy, Kimball O'Hara, who becomes involved in Secret Service activities in India; *Just So Stories,* a collection of nonsense tales, including *How The Elephant Got His Trunk* and *The Butterfly That Stamped; Puck of Pook's Hill* and its sequel *Rewards and Fairies,* in which two young children are magically taken back to different periods in English history; *Captains Courageous,* a sea story set among the cod fisheries of Newfoundland; and *Stalky & Co.,* a semi-autobiographical school story.

Rudyard Kipling died in 1936.

Rikki-Tikki-Tavi

by Rudyard Kipling

At the hole where he went in
　　Red-Eye called to Wrinkle-Skin.
Hear what little Red-Eye saith:
"Nag, come up and dance with death!"

Eye to eye and head to head,
　　(*Keep the measure, Nag.*)
This shall end when one is dead;
　　(*At thy pleasure, Nag.*)

Turn for turn and twist for twist—
　　(*Run and hide thee, Nag.*)
Hah! The hooded Death has missed!
　　(*Woe betide thee, Nag!*)

This is the story of the great war that Rikki-tikki-tavi fought single-handed, through the bathrooms of the big bungalow in Segowlee cantonment. Darzee, the tailor-bird, helped him, and Chuchundra, the muskrat, who never comes out into the middle of the floor, but always creeps round by the wall, gave him advice; but Rikki-tikki did the real fighting.

He was a mongoose, rather like a little cat in his fur and his tail, but quite like a weasel in his head and his habits. His eyes and the end of his restless nose were pink; he could scratch himself anywhere he pleased, with any leg, front or back, that he chose to use; he could fluff up his tail till it looked like a bottle-brush, and his war-cry as he scuttled through the long grass, was: *"Rikk-tikk-tikki-tikki-tchk!"*

One day, a high summer flood washed him out of the burrow where he lived with his father and mother, and carried him, kicking and clucking, down a roadside ditch. He found a little wisp of grass floating there, and clung to it till he lost his senses. When he revived, he was lying in the hot sun on the middle of a garden path, very draggled indeed, and a small boy was saying: "Here's a dead mongoose. Let's have a funeral."

"No," said his mother; "let's take him in and dry him. Perhaps he isn't really dead."

They took him into the house, and a big man picked him up between his fingers and thumb and said he was not dead but half choked; so they wrapped him in cotton wool, and warmed him, and he opened his eyes and sneezed.

"Now," said the big man (he was an Englishman who had just moved into the bungalow); "don't frighten him, and we'll see what he'll do."

It is the hardest thing in the world to frighten a mongoose, because he is eaten up from nose to tail with curiosity. The motto of all the mongoose family is, "Run and find out"; and Rikki-tikki was a true mongoose. He looked at the cotton wool, decided that it was not good to eat, ran all round the table, sat up and put his fur in order, scratched himself, and jumped on the small boy's shoulder.

"Don't be frightened, Teddy," said his father. "That's his way of making friends."

"Ouch! He's tickling under my chin," said Teddy.

Rikki-tikki looked down between the boy's collar and neck, snuffed at his ear, and climbed down to the floor, where he sat rubbing his nose.

"Good gracious," said Teddy's mother, "and that's a wild creature! I suppose he's so tame because we've been kind to him."

"All mongooses are like that," said her husband. "If Teddy doesn't pick him up by the tail, or try to put him in a cage, he'll run in and out of the house all day long. Let's give him something to eat."

They gave him a little piece of raw meat. Rikki-tikki liked it immensely, and when it was finished he went out into the veranda and sat in the sunshine and fluffed up his fur to make it dry to the roots. Then he felt better.

"There are more things to find out about in this house," he said to himself, "than all my family could find out in all their lives. I shall certainly stay and find out."

He spent all that day roaming over the house. He nearly drowned himself in the bath-tubs, put his nose into the ink on a writing-table, and burned it on the end of the big man's cigar, for he climbed up in the big man's lap to see how writing was done. At nightfall he ran into Teddy's nursery to watch how kerosene lamps were lighted, and when Teddy went to bed Rikki-tikki climbed up, too; but he was a restless companion, because he had to get up and attend to every noise all through the night, and find out what made it. Teddy's mother and father came in, the last thing, to look at their boy, and Rikki-tikki was awake on the pillow. "I don't like that," said Teddy's mother; "he may bite the child." "He'll do no such thing," said the father. "Teddy's safer with that little beast than if he had a bloodhound to watch him. If a snake came into the nursery now———"

But Teddy's mother wouldn't think of anything so awful.

Early in the morning Rikki-tikki came to early breakfast in the veranda riding on Teddy's shoulder, and they gave him banana and some boiled egg; and he sat on all their laps one after the other, because every well-brought-up mongoose always hopes to be a house-mongoose some day and have rooms to run about in, and Rikki-tikki's mother (she used to live in the General's house at Segowlee) had carefully told Rikki what to do if ever he came across white men.

Then Rikki-tikki went out into the garden to see what was to be seen. It was a large garden, only half cultivated, with bushes as big as summer-houses of Marshal Niel roses, lime and orange trees, clumps of bamboo, and thickets of high grass. Rikki-tikki licked his lips. "This is a splendid hunting-ground," he said, and his tail grew bottle-brushy at the thought of it, and he scuttled up and down the garden, snuffing here and there till he heard very sorrowful voices in a thorn-bush.

It was Darzee, the tailor-bird, and his wife. They had made a beautiful nest by pulling two big leaves together and stitching them up the edges with fibres, and had filled the hollow with cotton and downy fluff. The nest swayed to and fro, as they sat on the rim and cried.

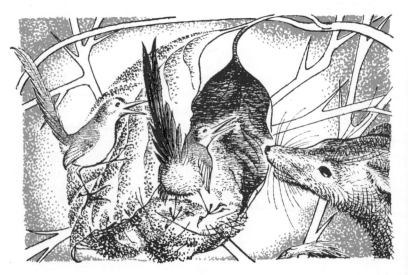

"What is the matter?" asked Rikki-tikki.

"We are very miserable," said Darzee. "One of our babies fell out of the nest yesterday and Nag ate him."

"H'm!" said Rikki-tikki, "that is very sad—but I am a stranger here. Who is Nag?"

Darzee and his wife only cowered down in the nest without answering, for from the thick grass at the foot of the bush there came a low hiss—a horrid cold sound that made Rikki-tikki jump back two clear feet. Then inch by inch out of the grass rose up the head and spread hood of Nag, the big black cobra, and he was five feet long from tongue to tail. When he had lifted one-third of himself clear of the ground, he stayed balancing to and fro exactly as a dandelion-tuft balances in the wind, and he looked at Rikki-tikki with the wicked snake's eyes that never change their expression, whatever the snake may be thinking of.

"Who is Nag?" he said. "*I* am Nag. The great god Brahm put his mark upon all our people when the first cobra spread his hood to keep the sun off Brahm as he slept. Look, and be afraid!"

He spread out his hood more than ever, and Rikki-tikki saw the spectacle-mark on the back of it that looks exactly like the eye part of a hook-and-eye fastening. He was afraid for the minute; but it is impossible for a mongoose to stay frightened for any length of time, and though Rikki-tikki had never met a live cobra before, his mother had fed him on dead ones, and he knew that all a grown mongoose's business in life was to fight and eat snakes. Nag knew that, too, and at the bottom of his cold heart he was afraid.

"Well," said Rikki-tikki, and his tail began to fluff up again, "marks or no marks, do you think it is right for you to eat fledglings out of a nest?"

Nag was thinking to himself, and watching the least little movement in the grass behind Rikki-tikki. He knew that mongooses in the garden meant death sooner or later for him and his family; but he wanted to get Rikki-tikki off his guard. So he dropped his head a little, and put it on one side.

"Let us talk," he said. "You eat eggs. Why should not I eat birds?"

"Behind you! Look behind you!" sang Darzee.

Rikki-tikki knew better than to waste time in staring. He jumped up in the air as high as he could go, and just under him whizzed by the head of Nagaina, Nag's wicked wife. She had crept up behind him as he was talking, to make an end of him; and he heard her savage hiss as the stroke missed. He came down almost across her back, and if he had been an old mongoose he would have known that then was the time to break her back with one bite; but he was afraid of the terrible lashing return-stroke of the cobra. He bit, indeed, but did not bite long enough, and he jumped clear of the whisking tail, leaving Nagaina torn and angry.

"Wicked, wicked Darzee!" said Nag, lashing up as high as he could reach towards the nest in the thorn-bush; but Darzee had built it out of reach of snakes, and it only swayed to and fro.

Rikki-tikki felt his eyes growing red and hot (when a mongoose's eyes grow red, he is angry), and he sat back on his tail and hind legs like a little kangaroo, and looked all around him, and chattered with rage. But Nag and Nagaina had disappeared into the grass. When a snake misses its stroke, it never says anything or gives any sign of what it means to do next. Rikki-tikki did not care to follow them, for he did not feel sure that he could manage two snakes at once. So he trotted off to the gravel path near the house, and sat down to think. It was a serious matter for him.

If you read the old books of natural history, you will find they say that when the mongoose fights the snake and happens to get bitten, he runs off and eats some herb that cures it. That is not true. The victory is only a matter of quickness of eye and quickness of foot—snake's blow against mongoose's jump—and as no eye can follow the motion of a snake's head when it strikes, that makes things much more wonderful than any magic herb. Rikki-tikki knew he was a young mongoose, and it made him all the more pleased to think he had managed to escape a blow from behind. It gave him confidence in himself and when Teddy came running down the path, Rikki-tikki was ready to be petted.

But just as Teddy was stopping, something flinched a little in the dust, and a tiny voice said: "Be careful. I am death!" It was Karait, the dusty brown snakeling that lies for choice on the dusty earth; and his bite is as dangerous as the cobra's. But he is so small that nobody thinks of him, and so he does the more harm to people.

Rikki-tikki's eyes grew red again, and he danced up to Karait with the peculiar rocking, swaying motion that he had inherited from his family. It looks very funny, but it is so perfectly balanced a gait that you can fly off from it at any angle you please; and in dealing with snakes this is an advantage. If Rikki-tikki had only known, he was doing a much more dangerous thing than fighting Nag for Karait is so small, and can turn so quickly, that unless Rikki bit him close to the back of the head, he would get the return-stroke in his eye or lip. But Rikki did not know: his eyes were all red, and he rocked back and forth, looking for a good place to hold. Karait struck out. Rikki jumped sideways and tried to run in, but the wicked little dusty grey head lashed within a fraction of his shoulder, and he had to jump over the body, and the head followed his heels close.

Teddy shouted to the house: "Oh, look here! Our mongoose is killing a snake"; and Rikki-tikki heard a scream from Teddy's mother. His father ran out with a stick, but by the time he came up, Karait had lunged out once too far, and Rikki-tikki had sprung, jumped on the snake's back, dropped his head far between his fore legs, bitten as high up the back as he could get hold, and rolled away. That bite paralyzed Karait, and Rikki-tikki was just going to eat him up from the tail, after the custom of his family at dinner, when he remembered that a full meal makes a slow mongoose, and if he wanted all his strength and quickness ready, he must keep himself thin.

He went away for a dust-bath under the castor-oil bushes, while Teddy's father beat the dead Karait. "What is the use of that?" thought Rikki-tikki. "I have settled it all"; and then Teddy's mother picked him up from the dust and hugged him, crying that he had saved Teddy from death, and Teddy's father said that he was a providence, and Teddy looked on with big scared eyes. Rikki-tikki was rather amused at all the fuss, which, of course, he did not understand. Teddy's mother might just as well have petted Teddy for playing in the dust. Rikki was thoroughly enjoying himself.

That night, at dinner, walking to and fro among the wine-glasses on the table, he could have stuffed himself three times over with nice things; but he remembered Nag and Nagaina, and though it was very pleasant to be patted and petted by Teddy's mother and to sit on Teddy's shoulders, his eyes would get red from time to time, and he would go off into his long war-cry of *"Rikk-tikk-tikki-tikki-tchk!"*

Teddy carried him off to bed, and insisted on Rikki-tikki sleeping under his chin. Rikki-tikki was too well bred to bite or scratch, but as soon as Teddy was asleep he went off for his nightly walk around the house, and in the dark he ran up against Chuchundra, the muskrat, creeping round by the wall. Chuchundra is a broken-hearted little beast. He whimpers and cheeps all the night, trying to make up his mind to run into the middle of the room, but he never gets there.

"Don't kill me," said Chuchundra, almost weeping. "Rikki-tikki, don't kill me."

"Do you think a snake-killer kills muskrats?" said Rikki-tikki scornfully.

"Those who kill snakes get killed by snakes," said Chuchundra, more sorrowfully than ever. "And how am I to be sure that Nag won't mistake me for you some dark night?"

"There's not the least danger," said Rikki-tikki; "but Nag is in the garden, and I know you don't go there."

"My cousin, Chua, the rat, told me—" said Chuchundra, and then he stopped.

"Told you what?"

"H'sh! Nag is everywhere, Rikki-tikki. You should have talked to Chua in the garden."

"I didn't—so you must tell me. Quick Chuchundra, or I'll bite you!"

Chuchundra sat down and cried till the tears rolled off his whiskers. "I am a very poor man," he sobbed. "I never had spirit enough to run out into the middle of the room. H'sh! I mustn't tell you anything. Can't you *hear*, Rikki-tikki?"

Rikki-tikki listened. The house was as still as still, but he thought he could just catch the faintest *scratch-scratch* in the world—a noise as faint as that of a wasp walking on a window-pane—the dry scratch of snake's scales on brickwork.

"That's Nag or Nagaina," he said to himself, "and he is crawling into the bathroom sluice. You're right, Chuchundra; I should have talked to Chua."

He stole off to Teddy's bathroom, but there was nothing there, and then to Teddy's mother's bathroom. At the bottom of the smooth plaster wall there was a brick pulled out to make a sluice for the bathwater, and as Rikki-tikki stole in by the masonry curb where the bath is put, he heard Nag and Nagaina whispering together outside in the moonlight.

"When the house is emptied of people," said Nagaina to her husband, "*he* will have to go away, and then the garden will be our own again. Go in quietly, and remember that the big man who killed Karait is the first one to bite. Then come out and tell me, and we will hunt for Rikki-tikki together."

"But are you sure that there is anything to be gained by killing the people?" said Nag.

"Everything. When there were no people in the bungalow, did we have any mongoose in the garden? So long as the bungalow is empty, we are king and queen of the garden; and remember that as soon as our eggs in the melon-bed hatch (as they may tomorrow), our children will need room and quiet."

"I had not thought of that," said Nag. "I will go, but there is no need that we should hunt for Rikki-tikki afterward. I will kill the big man and his wife, and the child if I can, and come away quietly. Then the bungalow will be empty, and Rikki-tikki will go."

Rikki-tikki tingled all over with rage and hatred at this, and then Nag's head came through the sluice, and his five feet of cold body followed it. Angry as he was, Rikki-tikki was very frightened as he saw the size of the big cobra. Nag coiled himself up, raised his head, and looked into the bathroom in the dark, and Rikki could see his eyes glitter.

"Now, if I kill him here, Nagaina will know; and if I fight him on the open floor, the odds are in his favour. What am I to do?" said Rikki-tikki-tavi.

Nag waved to and fro, and then Rikki-tikki heard him drinking from the biggest water-jar that was used to fill the bath. "That is good," said the snake. "Now, when Karait was killed, the big man had a stick. He may have that stick still, but when he comes in to bathe in the morning he will not have a stick. I shall wait here till he comes. Nagaina—do you hear me?—I shall wait here in the cool till daytime."

There was no answer from outside, so Rikki-tikki knew Nagaina had gone away. Nag coiled himself down, coil by coil, round the bulge at the bottom of the water-jar, and Rikki-tikki stayed still as death. After an hour he began to move, muscle by muscle, towards the jar. Nag was asleep, and Rikki-tikki looked at his big back wondering which would be the best place for a good hold. "If I don't break his back at the first jump," said Rikki, "he still can fight; and if he fights—O Rikki!" He looked at the thickness of the neck below the hood, but that was too much for him; and a bite near the tail would only make Nag savage.

"It must be the head," he said at last; "the head above the hood; and, when I am once there, I must not let go."

Then he jumped. The head was lying a little clear of the water-jar, under the curve of it; and, as his teeth met, Rikki braced his back against the bulge of the red earthenware to hold down the head. This gave him just one second's purchase, and he made the most of it. Then he was battered to and fro as a rat is shaken by a dog—to and fro on the floor, up and down, and round in great circles; but his eyes were red, and he held on as the body cart-whipped over the floor, upsetting the tin dipper and the soap-dish and the flesh-brush, and banged against the tin side of the bath. As he held he closed his jaws tighter and tighter, for he made sure he would be banged to death, and, for the honour of his family, he preferred to be found with his teeth locked. He was dizzy, aching, and felt shaken to pieces when something went off like a thunderclap just behind him; a hot wind knocked him senseless and red fire singed his fur. The big man had been wakened by the noise, and had fired both barrels of a shot-gun into Nag just behind the hood.

Rikki-tikki held on with his eyes shut, for now he was quite sure he was dead; but the head did not move, and the big man picked him up and said: "It's the mongoose again, Alice; the little chap has saved *our* lives now." Then Teddy's mother came in with a very white face, and saw what was left of Nag, and Rikki-tikki dragged himself to Teddy's bedroom and spent half the rest of the night shaking himself tenderly to find out whether he really was broken into forty pieces, as he fancied.

When morning came he was very stiff, but well pleased with his doings. "Now I have Nagaina to settle with, and she will be worse than five Nags, and there's no knowing when the eggs she spoke of will hatch. Goodness! I must go and see Darzee," he said.

Without waiting for breakfast, Rikki-tikki ran to the thorn-bush where Darzee was singing a song of triumph at the top of his voice. The news of Nag's death was all over the garden, for the sweeper had thrown the body on the rubbish-heap.

"Oh, you stupid tuft of feathers!" said Rikki-tikki, angrily. "Is this the time to sing?"

"Nag is dead—is dead—is dead!" sang Darzee. "The valiant Rikki-tikki caught him by the head and held fast. The big man brought the bang-stick and Nag fell in two pieces! He will never eat my babies again."

"All that's true enough; but where's Nagaina?" said Rikki-tikki, looking carefully round him.

"Nagaina came to the bathroom sluice and called for Nag," Darzee went on; "and Nag came out on the end of a stick—the sweeper picked him up on the end of a stick and threw him upon the rubbish-heap. Let us sing about the great, the red-eyed Rikki-tikki!" and Darzee filled his throat and sang.

"If I could get up to your nest, I'd roll all your babies out!" said Rikki-tikki. "You don't know when to do the right thing at the right time. You're safe enough in your nest there, but it's war for me down here. Stop singing a minute, Darzee."

"For the great, the beautiful Rikki-tikki's sake I will stop," said Darzee. "What is it, O Killer of the terrible Nag?"

"Where is Nagaina, for the third time?"

"On the rubbish-heap by the stables, mourning for Nag. Great is Rikki-tikki with the white teeth."

"Bother my white teeth! Have you ever heard where she keeps her eggs?"

"In the melon-bed, on the end nearest the wall, where the sun strikes nearly all day. She had them there weeks ago."

"And you never thought it worth while to tell me? The end nearest the wall, you said?"

"Rikki-tikki, you are not going to eat her eggs?"

"Not eat exactly; no. Darzee, if you have a grain of sense you will fly off to the stables and pretend that your wing is broken, and let Nagaina chase you away to this bush! I must get to the melon-bed, and if I went there now she'd see me."

Darzee was a feather-brained little fellow who could never hold more than one idea at a time in his head; and just because he knew that Nagaina's children were born in eggs like his own, he didn't think at first that it was fair to kill them. But his wife was a sensible bird, and she knew that cobra's eggs meant young cobras later on; so she flew off from the nest, and left Darzee to keep the babies warm, and continue his song about the death of Nag. Darzee was very like a man in some ways.

She fluttered in front of Nagaina by the rubbish-heap, and cried out, "Oh, my wing is broken! The boy in the house threw a stone at me and broke it." Then she fluttered more desperately than ever.

Nagaina lifted up her head and hissed, "You warned Rikki-tikki when I would have killed him. Indeed and truly, you've chosen a bad place to be lame in." And she moved toward Darzee's wife, slipping along over the dust.

72

"The boy broke it with a stone!" shrieked Darzee's wife.

"Well! It may be some consolation to you when you're dead to know that I shall settle accounts with the boy. My husband lies on the rubbish-heap this morning, but before night the boy in the house will lie very still. What is the use of running away? I am sure to catch you. Little fool, look at me!"

Darzee's wife knew better than to do *that*, for a bird who looks at a snake's eyes gets so frightened that she cannot move. Darzee's wife fluttered on, piping sorrowfully, and never leaving the ground, and Nagaina quickened her pace.

Rikki-tikki heard them going up the path from the stables, and he raced for the end of the melon-patch near the wall. There, in the warm litter about the melons, very cunningly hidden, he found twenty-five eggs, about the size of a bantam's eggs, but with whitish skin instead of shell.

"I was not a day too soon," he said; for he could see the baby cobras curled up inside the skin, and he knew that the minute they were hatched they could each kill a man or a mongoose. He bit off the tops of the eggs as fast as he could, taking care to crush the young cobras, and turned over the litter from time to time to see whether he had missed any. At last there were only three eggs left, and Rikki-tikki began to chuckle to himself, when he heard Darzee's wife screaming.

"Rikki-tikki, I led Nagaina toward the house, and she has gone into the veranda, and—oh, come quickly—she means killing!"

Rikki-tikki smashed two eggs, and tumbled backward down the melon-bed with the third egg in his mouth, and scuttled to the veranda as hard as he could put foot to ground. Teddy and his mother and father were there at early breakfast; but Rikki-tikki saw that they were not eating anything. They sat stone-still, and their faces were white. Nagaina was coiled up on the matting by Teddy's chair, within easy striking distance of Teddy's bare leg, and she was swaying to and fro singing a song of triumph.

"Son of the big man that killed Nag," she hissed, "stay still. I am not ready yet. Wait a little. Keep very still, all you three. If you move I strike, and if you do not move I strike. Oh, foolish people, who killed my Nag!"

Teddy's eyes were fixed on his father, and all his father could do was to whisper, "Sit still, Teddy. You mustn't move. Teddy, keep still."

Then Rikki-tikki came up and cried: "Turn round, Nagaina; turn and fight!"

"All in good time," said she, without moving her eyes. "I will settle my account with *you* presently. Look at your friends, Rikki-tikki. They are still and white; they are afraid. They dare not move, and if you come a step nearer I strike."

"Look at your eggs," said Rikki-tikki, "in the melon-bed near the wall. Go and look, Nagaina."

The big snake turned half round, and saw the egg on the veranda. "Ah-h! Give it to me," she said.

Rikki-tikki put his paws one on each side of the egg, and his eyes were blood-red. "What price for a snake's egg? For a young cobra? For a young king-cobra? For the last—the very last of the brood? The ants are eating all the others down by the melon-bed."

Nagaina spun clear round, forgetting everything for the sake of the one egg; and Rikki-tikki saw Teddy's father shoot out a big hand, catch Teddy by the shoulder and drag him across the little table with the tea-cups, safe and out of reach of Nagaina.

"Tricked! Tricked! Tricked! *Rikk-tck-tck!*" chuckled Rikki-

tikki. "The boy is safe, and it was I—I—I that caught Nag by the hood last night in the bathroom." Then he began to jump up and down, all four feet together, his head close to the floor. "He threw me to and fro, but he could not shake me off. He was dead before the big man blew him in two. I did it. *Rikki-tikki-tck-tck!* Come then, Nagaina. Come and fight with me. You shall not be a widow long."

Nagaina saw that she had lost her chance of killing Teddy, and the egg lay between Rikki-tikki's paws. "Give me the egg, Rikki-tikki. Give me the last of my eggs, and I will go away and never come back," she said, lowering her hood.

"Yes, you will go away, and you will never come back; for you will go to the rubbish-heap with Nag. Fight, widow! The big man has gone for his gun! Fight!"

Rikki-tikki was bounding all round Nagaina, keeping just out of reach of her stroke, his little eyes like hot coals. Nagaina gathered herself together, and flung out at him. Rikki-tikki jumped up and backward. Again and again and again she struck, and each time her head came with a whack on the matting of the veranda and she gathered herself together like a watch-spring. Then Rikki-tikki danced in a circle to get behind her, and Nagaina spun round to keep her head to his head, so that the rustle of her tail on the matting sounded like dry leaves blown along by the wind.

He had forgotten the egg. It still lay on the veranda, and Nagaina came nearer and nearer to it, till at last, while Rikki-tikki was drawing breath, she caught it in her mouth, turned to the veranda steps, and flew like an arrow down the path, with Rikki-tikki behind her. When the cobra runs for her life, she goes like a whip-lash flicked across a horse's neck.

Rikki-tikki knew that he must catch her, or all the trouble would begin again. She headed straight for the long grass by the thorn-bush, and as he was running Rikki-tikki heard Darzee still singing his foolish little song of triumph. But Darzee's wife was wiser. She flew off her nest as Nagaina came along, and flapped her wings about Nagaina's head. If Darzee had helped they might have turned her; but Nagaina only lowered her hood and went on. Still, the instant's delay brought Rikki-tikki up to her, and as she plunged into the rat-hole where she and Nag used to live, his little white teeth were clenched on her tail, and he went down with her—and very few mongooses, however wise and old they may be, care to follow a cobra into its hole. It was dark in the hole; and Rikki-tikki never knew when it might open out and give Nagaina room to turn and strike at him. He held on savagely, and struck out his feet to act as brakes on the dark slope of the hot, moist earth.

Then the grass by the mouth of the hole stopped waving, and Darzee said: "It is all over with Rikki-tikki! We must sing his death-song. Valiant Rikki-tikki is dead! For Nagaina will surely kill him underground."

So he sang a mournful song that he made up all on the spur of the minute, and just as he got to the most touching part the grass quivered again, and Rikki-tikki, covered with dirt, dragged himself out of the hole leg by leg, licking his whiskers. Darzee stopped with a little shout. Rikki-tikki shook some of the dust out of his fur and sneezed. "It is all over," he said. "The widow will never come out again." And the red ants that live between the grass stems heard him, and began to troop down one after another to see if he had spoken the truth.

Rikki-tikki curled himself up in the grass and slept where he was—slept and slept till it was late in the afternoon, for he had done a hard day's work.

"Now," he said, when he awoke, "I will go back to the house. Tell the Coppersmith, Darzee, and he will tell the garden that Nagaina is dead."

The Coppersmith is a bird who makes a noise exactly like the beating of a little hammer on a copper pot; and the reason he is always making it is because he is the towncrier to every Indian garden, and tells all the news to everybody who cares to listen. As Rikki-tikki went up the path, he heard his "attention" notes like a tiny dinner-gong; and then the steady *"Ding-dong-tock!* Nag is dead—*dong!* Nagaina is dead! *Ding-dong-tock!"* That set all the birds in the garden singing, and the frogs croaking; for Nag and Nagaina used to eat frogs as well as little birds.

When Rikki got to the house, Teddy and Teddy's mother (she looked very white still, for she had been fainting) and Teddy's father came out and almost cried over him; and that night he ate all that was given him till he could eat no more, and went to bed on Teddy's shoulder, where Teddy's mother saw him when she came to look late at night.

"He saved our lives and Teddy's life," she said to her husband. "Just think, he saved all our lives."

Rikki-tikki woke up with a jump, for all the mongooses are light sleepers.

"Oh, it's you," said he. "What are you bothering for? All the cobras are dead; and if they weren't I'm here."

Rikki-tikki had a right to be proud of himself; but he did not grow too proud, and he kept that garden as a mongoose should keep it, with tooth and jump and spring and bite, till never a cobra dared show its head inside the walls.

DARZEE'S CHAUNT

(SUNG IN HONOUR OF RIKKI-TIKKI-TAVI)

Singer and tailor am I—
Doubled the joys that I know—
Proud of my lilt through the sky,
Proud of the house that I sew—
Over and under, so weave I my music—so weave I the house that I sew.

Sing to your fledglings again,
Mother, oh lift up your head!
Evil that plagued us is slain,
Death in the garden lies dead.
Terror that hid in the roses is impotent—flung on the dunghill and dead!

Who hath delivered us, who?
Tell me his nest and his name.
Rikki, the valiant, the true,
Tikki, with eyeballs of flame.
Rik-tikki-tikki, the ivory-fanged, the hunter with eyeballs of flame.

Give him the Thanks of the Birds,
Bowing with tail-feathers spread!
Praise him with nightingale words—
Nay, I will praise him instead.
Hear! I will sing you the praise of the bottle-tailed Rikki, with eyeballs of red!

(Here Rikki-tikki interrupted, and the rest of the song is lost.)

Colin Thiele

Colin Thiele was born in 1920 at Eudunda in South Australia. He was educated at various country schools, went to Adelaide University and during the Second World War served in the Royal Australian Air Force. After the war he became a teacher and has remained in education ever since.

He has scripted material for radio and television, written fact and fiction for adults, lectured on Australian literature, edited anthologies of verse, drama and prose and produced several volumes of poetry. It is for his children's stories, however, that he is best known. These provide not only humour, as in THE FISH SCALES, but evocative description and a strong sense of drama, of which THE SHELL is a good example. Both these stories are taken from *The Rim of The Morning,* which also contains *Storm Boy.* This moving tale of a young boy who befriends a pelican has been made into a film.

Sun on the Stubble – a comedy of Australian farm life – tells of a boy's last year in the country before going to secondary school in the city. *February Dragon* deals with the ever-present danger of bush fires in Australia. *Blue Fin* is about tuna fishing (Colin Thiele has sailed with the tuna fleets in South Australia) and the adventures of an unfortunate ugly duckling of a boy called Snook. Tall, clumsy, ungainly, it is only as a last resort that he is taken along as a crew member on his father's tuna clipper. When disaster strikes, Snook and his badly injured father are left alone on the battered vessel and it is up to Snook to save their lives, their boat and their cargo.

The Fish Scales

by Colin Thiele

The sea looked as if it wanted you to walk on it. Daybreak was setting the swell with a crust of light, hard and smooth, like milky chalcedony. You wanted to sit down in it and slide over the undulations till your pants were shiny, or toboggan into the troughs just for the fast, free shoot of it.

Tim and I sat on the engine-hatch with our lines out, facing east.

"Like a baker painting the top of a bun," he said.

"Some bun!"

He looked towards the horizon for a bit. It was far off across the rolling plain, fine as onyx.

"Yeah."

"Going to be some fishin' day, too. Perfect!"

"Perfect." Tim pulled in his line and the stone turned to water for a second, herringboned with tiny ripples.

"Daybreak on a cutter out at sea," said Tim. "You've got to see it."

"Yeah, when it's like this."

"Back in Port Lincoln they'll still be snoring holes in their pillows; they probably live half their lives within ten miles of this, and never know."

It was true. Port Lincoln was over the horizon; it was in the next valley. The plain of the sea flowed over the coast, just as the tide of light flowed over the sea. And with it came colour, till the cutter stood up in a pink smooth world, exquisite as the underbelly of a shell.

"Time to go below," said Tim. "Coming?"

"No. I'll fish for a bit."

"I'll whack up the breakfast, then, and see how poor old Bill's getting on; he was crook as a squirting squid last night."

"Right. I'll be down later."

In a way I was glad to be left alone. The truth was that I hadn't been doing too well with the line lately and I wanted to get in a few on the quiet to build up my tally. We were on snapper ground and I knew that if they got on the bite at daybreak I might run up a few.

But I wasn't ready, of course, for what happened: thud! Like a punch to the jaw.

My head flew back and I felt the rick in my neck. The armbone stretched away from the shoulder-blade an inch or two, but luckily my muscles and tendons were pretty elastic; they gave and then took up again. I felt sure I'd hooked a shark or a porpoise or maybe a fifteen-hand sea-horse. Twice he nearly had me over the side when he made a run for it. But I held him. Gradually I worked him up nearer the surface until I could see his outline dimly through the water.

Suffering catfish—the shape of him! He was five feet long! King of all king snapper, with a hump on him like a camel's. In the end I had him right up, just an inch or two below the surface, cruising around as quiet as you like. But it unnerved me just to look at him there—red and coral pink and pearl, gleaming and shining.

But there didn't seem to be any hope of getting him into the boat. I couldn't keep on playing him like this for long, and I didn't want to yell to the others in case I frightened him. Anyway, there was nothing they could have done to help, and I had my pride to think of. I wanted more than anything to surprise them when they came up; you know the sort of nonchalant modesty: "Any luck?"—"Just middling, not a bad snapper over there by the engine-hatch."

Finally I decided to risk everything on the one pull to draw him up over the side and spill him on to the decking. As long as the line held for the first half of the heave when he came up, I might do it, because if it broke then, he'd probably keep coming and fall into the boat anyway. That was usually the way of it. So I braced myself against the winch-head and with a couple of turns wound the line around my waist. Then I took a short firm grip, paused for a deep breath, and *heaved*. My muscles cracked and my eyes bulged.

I didn't know my own strength. In that tremendous pull he came straight up out of the sea like a hunting barracuda until there was only a foot of him left in the water. And in that instant he gave a flick of his great tail like Moby Dick, that hurled him clean out of the sea—that, and the pull I gave.

He shot up over my shoulder in a high curve like a tuna coming aboard, but the impulse of my jerk and his own tail-flip were stronger even than the toss of a tuna pole; he went up, up, over the crosstree of the mast, and then down, leaving the line threaded neatly over the arm.

And so, before I could foresee it, whang, the slack was all taken up and I was lifted off my feet with a jerk as quick as a pistol shot.

There I dangled, exactly balancing the fish, my feet a yard above the deck, treading and kicking the empty air. We were the perfect counterpoise; neither of us could pull the other down. And I'm twelve stone. That'll give you some idea of his weight.

The worst of it was that we didn't hang still. He kept jiggling about, twisting and turning, and I was scrabbling my hardest, too. Naturally, I was trying to weigh my side down; I didn't want him hauling me up towards the crosstrees like a flag at half-mast. So we got to swinging inwards and out, towards one another and away.

One minute I'd be trying ineffectually to embrace his slippery body, and his big wet eye would be staring right into mine; and then we'd swing apart like a couple of contrapendulums, squirming and wheezing before we slapped together again. Then for a change we'd spin round and round in a dizzy whirl, plaiting up the line above us. Face to face and back to back we'd spin, his fins giving me a few short jabs to the ribs, and my elbows getting him a jolt in the gills.

If you've ever been plaited up you know how helplessly frustrated it leaves you; wrapped up like a mummy swaddled in strip bandages. But to be plaited with a twelve-stone fish! It presses your face so hard into his that it's like waltzing with a bear-hugging partner—you can't converse properly because you can't get your head back far enough to see him objectively. At any

rate, that's how it went with us until we unplaited ourselves and flew apart again.

Luckily, I managed to slow things down after a while by clutching at the mast whenever I shot past, until we finally stopped spinning and just swung backwards and forwards again like a pendulum in an old grandfather clock. Yet that's when the crisis came.

On the second or third swing I could see by the look on his face that he thought he might still have the better of me, and sure enough, the next time we came towards one another he twisted up his powerful tail and fetched me a whack in the stomach, way below the belt, that took the wind out of me with a *wup*. And while I was dangling limp as a gibbet corpse he took his mean advantage, screwed himself right up till he was nearly lying sideways in the air, and gave me a slap on the side of the head that sent my false teeth skidding into the engine-well.

I tell you it's no joke to be slapped in the face by a twelve-stone snapper. It just about did for me. Through the haze I could see half a dozen five-foot fish overlapping and vibrating like a plucked harp-string, and I knew that if he fetched me one more clout like that he'd take me and finish up leaning against the mast himself, playing me on the end of *his* line.

So I made the effort somehow; I had to. Luckily we missed each other altogether the next time, and swung past, hissing hate and looking back vindictively at each other over our shoulders. That gave me a momentary breather and I was half prepared on the next swing. Two can play at that game, I said, and just before we met I brought up my right thigh and kneed him neatly in the belly. A good, shady footballer's groin thrust.

It was his turn to go *wup*! That put some heart and wind back into me, and I was really ready the next time with a long punt kick that caught him in the paunch and sank in with a saggy squelch.

"How's that?" I said.

His eyes goggled glazily and he blew out a lazy string of bubbles. I could see that I was getting the upper hand. A few more swings and he'd be mine. Then, when he was hanging limp, I'd cut the line, we'd both drop to the deck, and I'd be able to display my catch as if nothing had happened.

The pride before the fall! Especially when you're up a mast with a fish. He had more life in him than I'd bargained for, because on the next swing, just as I was lifting my leg to give him the knockout, he caught his tail under my feet and flicked me back in a high wide arc like a squeezed pip.

Far out over the side of the boat I swung, and so did he. Action and reaction! My snapper line was a good one, but it wasn't made for bowing and sawing up in the crosstrees. It had been fraying slowly all the time, and now on the very end of that high outward swing it snapped, and the two of us flew on in a sort of sine-wave.

Same weight, same distance, same speed—we hit the water simultaneously. Down below they would just have heard the one splash.

When I came to the surface to cough, Tim was leaning over the rail, the tears of laughter running off him like bow-spray.

"He's thrown himself in," he yelled down to Bill. "I always said he would."

"I just hooked the biggest snapper alive," I yelled, "but he got away."

Tim was whooping with delight.

"He tied the line round his waist and threw so hard that he tossed himself in."

I climbed aboard, sore and dripping. "He got away," I panted, "a two-hundred-pound snapper; had him aboard, had him right here, but he got away."

Tim looked at the bit of line trailing after me, eyeing the frayed end.

"'Struth, you must've given yourself a heave, sport," he said, "to bust a line like that."

"I tell you it was a fish that pulled me in," I said, "and by trickery at that. I was joined to him by the middle."

He raised one eyebrow. "Hey!" he yelled. "Come up here quick, Bill, and have a look at poor old Bert's umbilical cord."

And so it was that I lost my fish and my hooks, my sinkers and half my line. . . . Everything, in fact, except the shame of my story as they told it. *That* didn't get away.

C. S. Lewis

C. S. Lewis was born in 1898 in Belfast. His mother died when he was quite young and his childhood and youth were spent in various boarding schools, all of which he detested. He entered Oxford University in 1917 but enlisted soon afterwards in the British Army. Two years later, after being invalided out, he returned to Oxford, where he later became a don. In 1954 he became a professor at Cambridge University. He died in 1963.

He wrote seven books specifically for young readers, the first of which, *The Lion, the Witch and the Wardrobe*, appeared in 1950. In this story, four children enter the land of Narnia through the back of a wardrobe in the spare room of their house. Narnia is a mysterious kingdom dominated by the fight between good, represented by the great lion Aslan, and evil, usually controlled by a witch and her followers. The remaining books in the series tell how various other children enter Narnia and become involved in adventures there. If you wish to read the series in chronological order, you should start with *The Magician's Nephew*, followed by *The Lion, the Witch and the Wardrobe*, *The Horse and his Boy*, *Prince Caspian*, *The Voyage of the "Dawn Treader"*, *The Silver Chair* and *The Last Battle*.

Of his books for adults, you are most likely to enjoy the science-fiction trilogy consisting of *Out of the Silent Planet*, *Perelandra* and *That Hideous Strength*. The first story deals with a voyage to Mars, the second with a trip to Venus and the third is a kind of "spiritual thriller". Also worth trying is *Other Worlds*, from which FORMS OF THINGS UNKNOWN is taken.

Forms of Things Unknown

by C. S. Lewis

"Before the class breaks up, gentlemen," said the instructor, "I should like to make some reference to a fact which is known to some of you, but probably not yet to all. High Command, I need not remind you, has asked for a volunteer for yet one more attempt on the Moon. It will be the fourth. You know the history of the previous three. In each case the explorers landed unhurt; or at any rate alive. We got their messages. Every message short, some apparently interrupted. And after that never a word, gentlemen. I think the man who offers to make the fourth voyage has about as much courage as anyone I've heard of. And I can't tell you how proud it makes me that he is one of my own pupils. He is in this room at this moment. We wish him every possible good fortune. Gentlemen, I ask you to give three cheers for Lieutenant John Jenkin."

Then the class became a cheering crowd for two minutes; after that a hurrying, talkative crowd in the corridor. The two biggest cowards exchanged the various family reasons which had deterred them from volunteering themselves. The knowing man said, "There's something behind all this." The vermin said, "He always was a chap who'd do anything to get himself into the limelight." But most just shouted out, "Jolly good show, Jenkin," and wished him luck.

Ward and Jenkin got away together into a pub.

"You kept this pretty dark," said Ward. "What's yours?"

"A pint of draught Bass," said Jenkin.

"Do you want to talk about it?" said Ward rather awkwardly when the drinks had come. "I mean—if you won't think I'm butting in, it's not just because of that girl, is it?"

That girl was a young woman who was thought to have treated Jenkin rather badly.

"Well," said Jenkin, "I don't suppose I'd be going if she had married me. But it's not a spectacular attempt at suicide or any rot of that sort. I'm not depressed. I don't feel anything particular about her. Not much interested in women at all, to tell you the truth. Not now. A bit petrified."

"What is it then?"

"Sheer unbearable curiosity. I've read those three little messages over and over till I know them by heart. I've heard every theory there is about what interrupted them. I've——"

"Is it certain they were all interrupted? I thought one of them was supposed to be complete."

"You mean Traill and Henderson? I think it was as incomplete as the others. First there was Stafford. He went alone, like me."

"Must you? I'll come, if you'll have me."

Jenkin shook his head. "I know you would," he said. "But you'll see in a moment why I don't want you to. But to go back to the messages. Stafford's was obviously cut short by something. It went *Stafford from within 50 miles of Point X0308 on the Moon. My landing was excellent. I have*—then silence. Then come Traill and Henderson. *We have landed. We are perfectly well. The ridge M392 is straight ahead of me as I speak. Over.*"

"What do you make of *Over*?"

"Not what you do. You think it means *finis*—the message is over. But who in the world, speaking to Earth from the Moon for the first time in all history, would have so little to say—if he *could* say any more? As if he'd crossed to Calais and sent his grandmother a card to say, 'Arrived safely'. The thing's ludicrous."

"Well, what do *you* make of *Over*?"

"Wait a moment. The last lot were Trevor, Woodford, and Fox. It was Fox who sent the message. Remember it?"

"Probably not so accurately as you."

"Well, it was this. *This is Fox speaking. All has gone*

90

wonderfully well. A perfect landing. You shot pretty well for I'm on Point X0308 at this moment. Ridge M392 straight ahead. On my left, far away across the crater I see the big peaks. On my right I see the Yerkes cleft. Behind me. Got it?"

"I don't see the point."

"Well, Fox was cut off the moment he said *Behind me.* Supposing Traill was cut off in the middle of saying, "Over my shoulder I can see" or "Over behind me" or something like that?"

"You mean ... ?"

"All the evidence is consistent with the view that everything went well till the speaker looked behind him, then something got him."

"What sort of a something?"

"That's what I want to find out. One idea in my head is this. Might there be something on the Moon—or something psychological about the experience of landing on the Moon—which drives men fighting mad?"

"I see. You mean Fox looked round just in time to see Trevor and Woodford preparing to knock him on the head?"

"Exactly. And Traill—for it was Traill—just in time to see Henderson a split second before Henderson murdered him. And that's why I'm not going to risk having a companion; least of all my best friend."

"This doesn't explain Stafford."

"No. That's why one can't rule out the other hypothesis."

"What is it?"

"Oh, that whatever killed them all was something they found there. Something lunar."

"You're surely not going to suggest life on the Moon at this time of day?"

"The word *life* always begs the question. Because, of course, it suggests organization as we know it on Earth—with all the chemistry which organization involves. Of course there could hardly be anything of that sort. But there might—I at any rate can't say there couldn't—be masses of matter capable of movements determined from within, determined, in fact, by intentions."

"Oh Lord, Jenkin, that's nonsense. Animated stones, no doubt! That's mere science fiction or mythology."

"Going to the Moon at all was once science fiction. And as for mythology, haven't they found the Cretan labyrinth?"

"And all it really comes down to," said Ward, "is that no one has ever come back from the Moon, and no one, so far as we know, ever survived there for more than a few minutes. Damn the whole thing." He stared gloomily into his tankard.

"Well," said Jenkin cheerily. "Somebody's got to go. The whole human race isn't going to be licked by any blasted satellite."

"I might have known that was your real reason," said Ward.

"Have another pint and don't look so glum," said Jenkin. "Anyway, there's loads of time. I don't suppose they'll get me off for another six months at the earliest."

But there was hardly any time. Like any man in the modern world on whom tragedy has descended or who has undertaken a high enterprise, he lived for the next few months a life not unlike that of a hunted animal. The Press, with all their cameras and notebooks, were after him. They did not care in the least whether he was allowed to eat or sleep or whether they made a nervous wreck of him before he took off. "Flesh-flies," he called them. When forced to address them, he always said, "I wish I could take you all with me." But he reflected also that a Saturn's ring of dead (and burnt) reporters circling round his space-ship might get on his nerves. They would hardly make "the silence of those eternal spaces" any more homelike.

The take-off when it came was a relief. But the voyage was worse than he had ever anticipated. Not physically—on that side it was nothing worse than uncomfortable—but in the emotional experience. He had dreamed all his life, with mingled terror and longing, of those eternal spaces; of being utterly "outside", in the sky. He had wondered if the agoraphobia of that roofless and bottomless vacuity would overthrow his reason. But the moment he had been shut into his ship there descended upon him the suffocating knowledge that the real danger of space-travel is claustrophobia. You have been put in a little metal container; somewhat like a cupboard, very like a coffin. You can't see out; you can see things only on the screen. Space and the stars are just as remote as they were on the Earth. Where you are is always your world. The sky is never where you are. All you have done is to exchange a large world of earth and rock and water and clouds for a tiny world of metal.

This frustration of a life-long desire bit deeply into his mind as the cramped hours passed. It was not, apparently, so easy to jump out of one's destiny. Then he became conscious of another motive which, unnoticed, had been at work on him when he volunteered. That affair with the girl had indeed frozen him stiff; petrified him, you might say. He wanted to feel again, to be flesh, not stone. To feel anything, even terror. Well, on this trip there would be terrors enough before all was done. He'd be wakened, never fear. That part of his destiny at least he felt he could shake off.

The landing was not without terror, but there were so many gimmicks to look after, so much skill to be exercised, that it did not amount to very much. But his heart was beating a little more noticeably than usual as he put the finishing touches to his space-suit and climbed out. He was carrying the transmission apparatus with him. It felt, as he had expected, as light as a loaf. But he was not going to send any message in a hurry. That might be where all the others had gone wrong. Anyway, the longer he waited the longer those press-men would be kept out of their beds waiting for their story. Do 'em good.

The first thing that struck him was that his helmet had been too lightly tinted. It was painful to look at all in the direction of the sun. Even the rock—it was, after all, rock not dust (which disposed of one hypothesis)—was dazzling. He put down the apparatus; tried to take in the scene.

The surprising thing was how small it looked. He thought he could account for this. The lack of atmosphere forbade nearly all the effects that distance has on Earth. The serrated boundary of the crater was, he knew, about twenty-five miles away. It looked as if you could have touched it. The peaks looked as if they were a few feet high. The black sky, with its inconceivable multitude and ferocity of stars, was like a cap forced down upon the crater; the stars only just out of his reach. The impression of a stage-set in a toy theatre, therefore of something arranged, therefore of something waiting for him, was at once disappointing and oppressive. Whatever terrors there might be, here, too, agoraphobia would not be one of them.

He took his bearings and the result was easy enough. He was, like Fox and his friends, almost exactly on Point X0308. But there was no trace of human remains.

If he could find any, he might have some clue as to how they died. He began to hunt. He went in each circle further from the ship. There was no danger of losing it in a place like this.

Then he got his first real shock of fear. Worse still, he could not tell what was frightening him. He only knew that he was engulfed in sickening unreality; seemed neither to be where he was nor to be doing what he did. It was also somehow connected with an experience long ago. It was something that had happened in a cave. Yes; he remembered now. He had been walking along supposing himself alone and then noticed that there was always a sound of other feet following him. Then in a flash he realized what was wrong. This was the exact reverse of the experience in the cave. Then there had been too many footfalls. Now there were too few. He walked on hard rock as silently as a ghost. He swore at himself for a fool—as if every child didn't know that a world without air would be a world without noise. But the silence, though explained, became none the less terrifying.

He had now been alone on the Moon for perhaps thirty-five minutes. It was then that he noticed the three strange things.

The sun's rays were roughly at right angles to his line of sight, so that each of the things had a bright side and a dark side; for each dark side a shadow like Indian ink lay out on the rock. He thought they looked like Belisha beacons. Then he thought they looked like huge apes. They were about the height of a man. They were indeed like clumsily shaped men. Except—he resisted an impulse to vomit—that they had no heads.

They had something instead. They were (roughly) human up to their shoulders. Then, where the head should have been, there was utter monstrosity—a huge spherical block; opaque, featureless. And every one of them looked as if it had that moment stopped moving or were at that moment about to move.

Ward's phrase about "animated stones" darted up hideously from his memory. And hadn't he himself talked of something that we couldn't call life, not in our sense, something that could nevertheless produce locomotion and have intentions? Something which, at any rate, shared with life life's tendency to kill? If there were such creatures—mineral equivalents to organisms—they could probably stand perfectly still for a hundred years without feeling any strain.

Were they aware of him? What had they for senses? The opaque globes on their shoulders gave no hint.

There comes a moment in nightmare, or sometimes in real battle, when fear and courage both dictate the same course: to rush, planless, upon the thing you are afraid of. Jenkin sprang upon the nearest of the three abominations and rapped his gloved knuckles against its globular top.

Ach!—he'd forgotten. No noise. All the bombs in the world might burst here and make no noise. Ears are useless on the Moon.

He recoiled a step and next moment found himself sprawling on the ground. "This is how they all died," he thought.

But he was wrong. The figure above him had not stirred. He was quite undamaged. He got up again and saw what he had tripped over.

It was a purely terrestrial object. It was, in fact, a transmission set. Not exactly like his own, but an earlier and supposedly inferior model—the sort Fox would have had.

As the truth dawned on him an excitement very different from that of terror seized him. He looked at their mis-shaped bodies; then down at his own limbs. Of course; that was what one looked like in a space suit. On his own head there was a similar monstrous globe, but fortunately not an opaque one. He was looking at three statues of spacemen: at statues of Trevor, Woodford, and Fox.

But then the moon must have inhabitants; and rational inhabitants; more than that, artists.

And what artists! You might quarrel with their taste, for no line anywhere in any of the three statues had any beauty. You could not say a word against their skill. Except for the head and face inside each headpiece, which obviously could not be attempted in such a medium, they were perfect. Photographic accuracy had never reached such a point on Earth. And though they were

95

faceless you could see from the set of their shoulders, and indeed of their whole bodies, that a momentary pose had been exactly seized. Each was the statue of a man turning to look behind him. Months of work had doubtless gone to the carving of each; it caught that instantaneous gesture like a stone shapshot.

Jenkin's idea was now to send his message at once. Before anything happened to himself, Earth must hear this amazing news. He set off in great strides, and presently in leaps—now first enjoying lunar gravitation—for his ship and his own set. He was happy now. He *had* escaped his destiny. Petrified, eh? No more feelings? Feelings enough to last him forever.

He fixed the set so that he could stand with his back to the sun. He worked the gimmicks. "Jenkin, speaking from the Moon," he began.

His own huge black shadow lay out before him. There is no noise on the Moon. Up from behind the shoulders of his own shadow another shadow pushed its way along the dazzling rock. It was that of a human head. And what a head of hair. It was all rising, writhing—swaying in the wind perhaps. Very thick the hairs looked. Then, as he turned in terror, there flashed through his mind the thought, "But there's no wind. No air. It can't be *blowing* about." His eyes met hers.

Henry Lawson

Henry Lawson was born in 1876 on the gold diggings near Grenfell in New South Wales. His father was a Norwegian sailor turned carpenter, his mother a strong-minded Australian with very definite views on democracy and the rights of women. At the age of fourteen he began work as a carpenter, the first of many jobs.

When his parents separated, he followed his mother to Sydney and began to write articles and poetry for newspapers and magazines, including one run by his mother. From her he inherited not only his desire to write but also his socialist views; during the shearers' strike in 1890 he wrote poems in support of the strikers. Always a solitary, unsettled man, he wandered about the thinly populated Australian outback in the depression years of the early 1890s, gaining many insights into the character of the Australian bushman.

He married in 1896 and went to live in Perth, where he wrote some of his best stories. But he was lonely and unhappy and after a few years made his way back to Sydney, as he also did at three later periods in his life – after working in a little Maori school in New Zealand, after three years as an author in London, and after a spell on a government farm in New South Wales. He died in 1922.

He wrote a large number of articles, poems and novels, but it is for his short stories that he is best remembered, particularly those in *When the Billy Boils, On the Track and Over the Sliprails* and *Joe Wilson and his Mates*. WAGGING IT and THE IRON-BARK CHIP are both good examples of his humour and his understanding of life in the Australian bush.

Wagging It

by Henry Lawson

That's what we called "playing truant".

Bill and Jim and Joe went to the old bark school, through Long Gully and over the Gap, together. Jim was a bad boy; Bill was an easy-going boy, who mostly followed in Jim's lead; Joe was a good boy, and consequently a great nuisance to himself and his chums.

Our ambition was to fall a large tree. We'd work like negroes for days together, with tomahawks and blunt axes, and break many axe-handles, and risk hidings at home, and bread-and-water dinners, and canings and "keepings-in" at school, just to see a tree fall and hear it crash. We sawed and hacked down many sapplings, but they weren't satisfactory. We'd start a tree, and give it best, and tackle it again, until it became a standing danger, and some angry father came along and cut it down. And we'd hide round, if we could, and watch.

Bill and Joe, who were brothers, started off one morning, as usual, mounted bareback on an old grey horse. They generally met Jim when out of sight of home, and took him up behind; and sometimes the horse carried four boys to school if he could not manage to brush them off under one of the many low branches near the track. They had a big native apple-tree about half through, and were eager to finish it. This morning they met Jim at the foot of Long Gully, and he seemed surprised to see them, and said:

"Whereyer gointer?"

"School, of course. Ain't you?"

"Why there ain't no school!"

"How's that?"

"The missus's sick. I just seen Jimmy Nowlett, and he told me; so of course there won't be none."

"What's up with her?" asked Joe, innocently.

"Don't know—except that he's been married to her about a year. Anyway, there ain't no school; so come along and we'll fall that tree. Ain't yer glad?"

"We'd better go on and make sure first," said Joe, conscientiously.

"What's the use?" snapped Jim. "We'll only have to come back agin. I tell yer there ain't no school. Yer always frightened of doing something. What's the good of being so soft? Why, Jim Nowlett says yer only fit for kissing girls."

This insult caused a quarrel between Jim and Joe; but Bill interposed, and they shook hands and argued the school question again. Jim thought it was no use going now, anyway, as they were late already, and would be sure to "cop out on it". But Joe's big conscience wouldn't let him rest, so at last Jim said:

"Well, look here, I'll tell you what we'll do. We'll go along to the top of the gap. I can see the school from there"—nobody else could—"and, if there ain't no school, Mother Palmer'll be cleaning out the school-room for the dance they're going to have to-morrer night, and she'll have the blackboards out in the yard. We'll go and see if the boards is out, and that'll settle it."

The old grey was brought alongside a stump, and Jim mounted behind the other two. Near the gap they saw some girls on the other side of the gully, and Jim hailed them:

"Hello, girls! Where yer goin' ter?"

They didn't catch what he said, but one of them screamed back:

"Jest see if I don't tell the master jest as soon as I get to school, Jim Bullock. I know what you said, you dirty larrikin!" The others said: "O, O, O-o-o!" They evidently reckoned that Jim had said something "naughty".

They reached the gap. The school was now about a mile off, and nothing could be seen save the point of a gable above the trees. Jim slid to the ground, climbed a rock, and stood for a moment in the

attitude of a stage-scout on the look-out for "Injuns". Suddenly he simulated great joy, and yelled:

"Come along, boys! There ain't no school! I can see three blackboards!"

Joe: "Let me up."

Jim (losing all patience): "Wot for? You might as well call me a liar at once. Let Bill come; he's got stronger eyes than you."

Bill scrambled up and saw the boards also under Jim's directions, but not so distinctly as Jim did—besides, he only saw two. Joe couldn't see anything save the bit of gable aforesaid, but they blamed it to the weakness of his eyes—he had good eyes—and he decided to let the thing go by the vote of the majority.

They broke two axe-handles chopping down the "apple-tree", which fell on a squatter's fence and demolished several panels. They got hidings and bread-and-water at home, and they got caned and kept in at school—all through Jim's vivid imagination and instinctive knowledge of human nature.

But the tree made a grand crash.

Barbara Leonie Picard

Barbara Leonie Picard was born in 1917 in Richmond, Surrey, of mixed French and German-Venezuelan parentage. She was educated at a boarding-school in Berkshire.

"From an early age I intended to write, and, as a child, I frequently did so for my own amusement; but it was not until 1949 that my first book was published."

The book was a collection of original fairy tales, entitled *The Mermaid and the Simpleton*. After two more such collections and a number of volumes retelling traditional stories, she wrote her first full-length historical novel for young people, *Ransom for a Knight*. In this absorbing account of medieval times, two children travel the length of England to deliver a bag of jewels that is needed as ransom. In *Lost John,* young John Fitzwilliam is taken prisoner by a band of robbers in the Forest of Arden. He does not realise at the time what an important part their chief, Sir Ralf the Red, is to play in his life, nor how soon he will come face to face with his father's murderer, for whom he was searching when he was captured. *One is One* is about the hardships and grief experienced by fourteen-year-old Stephen de Beauville in his struggle to become a knight; while *The Young Pretenders* deals with the risks faced by two young supporters of the Stuart cause in the Jacobite rebellion. TOM TURNSPIT is set in the Elizabethan period.

Barbara Leonie Picard explains her approach to writing in straightforward terms:

"I still write as much for myself as for my readers and I could never write anything in which I was not personally interested."

Tom Turnspit

by Barbara Leonie Picard

There had been a state of simmering excitement in the castle kitchen ever since, in the late hours of the morning, one of the maidservants had run in, calling out that the players had come and were to perform in the great hall after supper. But when, later, my lord's steward had come to the kitchen to announce, in his usual self-important fashion, that my lord and lady had graciously given permission for all the castle servants to watch the play that evening, the excitement had risen to boiling within two minutes of his departure. After that, in the busy, bustling kitchen, the talk amongst the score of servants of every degree who worked there, had been of nothing but the players: for as a rule little entertainment ever came their way. First one of them and then another would be slipping out of the kitchen on some pretext or other, in the hope of catching a glimpse of the players, but with little success; though someone did claim to have seen two of them unloading from their cart one of the coffers which held whatever marvels it might be that players carried with them; while another swore to having seen their pony enjoying a well-earned rest and a feed in the castle stables.

It was so many years since a company of players had last visited the castle, that none of the younger servants had ever seen a play performed, and had little idea of what manner of folk players might be, or what form of entertainment they had to offer. Those of the older servants who claimed to have, at some time, seen players perform, and those others who professed to have more knowledge of the world found themselves being questioned avidly as to the ways and habits and appearance of players.

The most ignorant of all on the matter was undoubtedly the youngest and smallest of the scullions, Tom the foundling, whose task it was to keep the spits turning with the dozens of fowl and the huge joints that were set to roast each day before the wide fireplaces. Even in winter, when warmth was welcome, it was no comfortable labour: in summer it was a torment. And when Tom was not turning the spits he was kept busy with all those other unpleasant tasks which everyone always left to him. Tom Turnspit, small and lean, his skin scorched brown as a wandering Egyptian's from long exposure to the flames, was the butt of the younger and livelier servants and a scapegoat for all the rest.

The castle had been standing for about three hundred years, and the draughty great hall was on the first floor, above the huge kitchen. There was, of course, a comfortable modern wing, some fifty years old, with fine chambers for my lord and lady and their family, and a banqueting hall where, a good many years before Tom's unwanted birth, Queen Elizabeth the First had been entertained for three whole days at an all but ruinous cost. But

Tom had never set foot inside the new West Wing, and he could have counted on the fingers of two hands the times he had been in the great hall or any other upper room of the old building, and on the fingers of one hand the times that he had gone beyond the castle walls, to the nearby village with its church, its alehouse, and its watermill. For Tom's own world was bounded by the kitchen walls; within them he worked all day, and in a draughty corner, on a heap of straw and rags, he slept at night.

On this fine early autumn day he became aware of the players' arrival and saw the stir it caused, and he wondered at it, for he had never heard of folk called players and had no idea what they could be. He knew, though, that it would be useless for him to ask, for no one would bother to tell him; and it was more than likely that he would have his ears boxed for asking questions about matters which were not his concern. But he listened to what was being said all around him, and in this way he learnt several conflicting facts: that players were like mummers; that they were not, for they were different and far better than mummers; that they sang songs and begged for pence; that they did not sing, but told stories about kings and queens, and pretended to be those kings and queens while they were telling the stories; that they danced, wearing strange clothing, upon stilts and swords; that they did not dance but juggled instead with knives and balls and platters. Tom also overheard Simon, who was usually respected by all for being able to read and write, declare several times, forcibly and heatedly, to different people, that players were rogues and vagabonds who should be whipped from any place where they dared to show their brazen faces; but Tom decided that this might perhaps be discounted, since everyone else jeered at Simon for a scurvy, spoilsport puritan, who was talking nonsense.

It was all very bewildering to Tom, but also very marvellous; and when, along with the others, he heard from the lips of the steward himself that all the servants might see the players, he could hardly believe his luck. And, hardly believing it, he thought he would do best to make sure of it. Timidly he approached the head cook, who, fortunately, had seemed in a good mood all that morning, and asked if he, too, might see the players in the great hall. He was immediately afraid that he had been mistaken about the cook's mood, when he heard him bellow in reply, "What's that I hear? You, you idle brat, you want to see the players? Most certainly you shall not."

Though terrified, Tom's longing to see the players was such that he dared a second appeal. "But, please, sir, Master Bolton said my lord had told him all the servants might see the players. All of them, sir."

Tom had, in fact, not been mistaken. The cook was in a very good mood that morning. After glaring at Tom in silence for a full half-minute, so that Tom began to tremble, he burst into a loud guffaw. "So that's what my lord said, is it? 'All the servants and make sure that Tom Turnspit is not forgotten.' Lackwit, do you think my lord even knows there's an ugly brat named Tom in his kitchen? To be sure he does not! And if he has never heard of you, he cannot mean you to go to the great hall and see the players, can he?"

Poor Tom had no idea of how to answer this. Miserably he watched the cook begin to laugh again, heard others join in his mirth, and believed that all was lost. But when the cook had laughed his fill, he said, "Very well, Master Thomas Turnspit, valued servant of my lord, you shall see the players this evening—but only if you work hard and I can find no fault with you all day. Now be off with you and back to your tasks." He hurried Tom on his way with a clout, and Tom, incredulous and overjoyed, fled back to the spits.

Never one who dared to shirk, Tom surpassed even himself that day, working every second, and working enough for three; the whole time in spirits which had at one moment reached the heights of joyful anticipation, and at the next fell to despairing depths at the thought that he might in some way be found to have trespassed, and so lose the promised reward. But all went well, and at last the time came when the servants, in chattering groups, friend by cheerful friend, began to make their way to the great hall. Tom's heart was hammering with excitement, his eyes were bright with eagerness, and his whole being was alive with an unfamiliar emotion to which, had he been asked, he could not have given a name, since he had never before experienced happiness. He was making to follow three of the other lads from the kitchen—he would never have dared to join them and walk beside them, nor, indeed, would they have permitted it; and he was beneath the arch of the doorway when the head cook's voice roared out at him, "Tom, you good for nothing, where do you think you're going? Come here at once."

The cook's good mood had not lasted quite long enough. Not fifteen minutes before, he had fallen out with the cellarer and had had the worst of their argument; now he was looking for a victim on whom he might avenge his discomfiture. Upon Tom's stammered "You said I might see the players if you found no fault with me today, sir. You have not—" the cook broke in furiously, "And now I have changed my mind. The great hall is no place for a misbegotten beggar's brat. You shall stay here where you belong." He struck out at Tom and, his rancour somewhat appeased, strode away up to the great hall.

Tom hardly felt the blow which sent him sprawling, and he was unaware of the bruising flagstones on which he fell; all he knew, and all he could feel or think of, was that he would not see the players.

In the great hall of the castle, where at one end a stage had been improvised for the players, the play had begun. To Martin, in his role of the Good Angel, had been allotted the lines—Prologue, linking narratory passages and Epilogue—intended to be spoken by Chorus. At first, as he had stepped forward from behind the screens which had been set up to mask the players' entrances and conceal the archway to the back-stairs up which they had to come, he had been a little nervous: not afraid of failure—he was too certain of his skill for that—but cautious and ready to adapt his performance to the mood of the spectators, as was wise when facing an audience whose tastes and temper were unknown. Yet there had been no sign of tenseness as his first words had rung out confidently, and the sweet sound of his clear, high voice had filled the hall.

> Not marching in the fields of Thrasimene,
> Where Mars did mate the warlike Carthagens . . .

He did not fear the responsibility of being the one to speak the opening lines and set the play upon its course, for he enjoyed the challenge offered by his rivals for the spectators' attention: ale-mug or wine-cup, flirtatious wench or lovely lady, ribald jesting or scholarly discussion; and when he handed on an eager and receptive audience to the player who was the next to speak he rejoiced in the pride he could always feel in something well achieved.

By the time his tenth line had been spoken, he knew that he had all their eyes and ears: the spectators' attention was his to keep safely until the closing lines of the Prologue, ready to be handed over to Master Banbury.

> Nothing so sweet as magic is to him,
> Which he prefers before his chiefest bliss:
> And this the man that in his study sits.

As the beautiful tones fell silent there was noisy and appreciative applause. Martin bowed deeply and, before it ceased and the spectators could begin to comment amongst each other on his appearance and performance, and thus leave the player who followed him to win their attention all over again, he slipped

behind the screens to where Master Banbury, leader of the company of players, was waiting, garbed as a scholar, an open book in his hands. He nodded approvingly to Martin, whispered "Well done, lad," then paced gravely from behind the screens, reading in his book as he walked, and sat down upon the bench which had been placed ready for him, a pile of three or four more books set to one end of it, to represent a study. After reading a moment or two further, he looked up and started on his long first speech:

> Settle thy studies, Faustus, and begin
> To sound the depth of that thou wilt profess ...

The Tragical History of the Life and Death of Dr Faustus, by Christopher Marlowe, was away to a promising start.

A small chamber near the foot of the secondary stairway which twisted down from the end of the great hall had been allotted to the players as a tiring-room. In the confusion of costumes, properties and bodies half-clad or strangely bedizened, Martin, helped by Robin, the younger and smaller of the two other boys in the company, now attired as a devil, removed his angel's wig and halo, wings and white robe. Underneath he already had on the patched trunk-hose of Wagner, the poor scholar who was servant to Dr Faustus. In spite of extensive cuts to the text and the omission of a number of characters, everyone in the company except Master Banbury as Faustus and young Master Kenton—who was Martin's own especial friend among them all and was playing Mephistopheles—was obliged to take several parts. Martin himself, beside his combination of the roles of the Good Angel and Chorus, was playing Wagner, Helen of Troy and one of the Seven Deadly Sins. The playwright's not having made provision for quite such stringent economy in the presentation of his work, had brought about two extremely quick changes for Martin. To see him safely through these, Master Kenton, who had a turn for words, had augmented Marlowe's verse by the addition of some score or so, and a dozen, lines respectively—something which he was not infrequently called upon to do on behalf of one playwright or another.

While Martin was hurriedly putting on Wagner's threadbare scholar's coat he was also trying to answer everyone's questions as to how the Prologue had been received, and what opinion he had formed of the spectators, and a handful of other matters. His change completed, he told Robin to come with him up to the hall, bringing the Good Angel's costume, because the first of his two quickest changes was due to be made after his first short scene as Wagner, and there would be no time for climbing down the break-neck, twisting stairway to the tiring-room and up again. "I'll carry the wings, and you can bring the rest. And for heaven's sake take care you do not tangle the wig or set the halo awry while going up the stairs, you imp of Satan," he warned, his familiar appellation for Robin sounding, for once, appropriate. Robin grimaced horribly and put out his tongue, then skipped away neatly as Martin aimed a good-natured cuff at him. Picking up the Good

Angel's wings of canvas-covered framework sewn with hundreds of dyed or gilded hens' feathers, Martin noticed a loose feather hanging by a single thread: there was no time to deal with it now; it would have to be stitched when the costumes were repacked. In the doorway he turned back and called to Master Kenton. "Those stairs, Will, they are dark enough already. This piece goes on for ever: it will be as black as the pit on the stairway long before we're done. We'll need torches if we are not to break our necks hurrying on them."

Master Kenton, knotting a cord around the Greyfriar's habit which was Mephistopheles' disguise, grinned and waved a hand at him. "I'll see to it. Now, for the love of heaven, make haste, or you'll miss your cue. Good luck!"

Martin did not miss his cue; moreover, aided by Robin, he managed his change back to the Good Angel in a remarkably short time, all things considered.

The play progressed, well received by the spectators at every point, and neared its closing scenes. Torches were lit and set around the now darkening hall. During another rapid change behind the screens Martin donned a farthingale and a very handsome—even if a trifle worn—gown of crimson brocade over Wagner's hose. Around his neck was a starched ruffle, on his head a gilt crown atop a wig of the popular saffron shade; while from his shoulders hung the silver-embroidered velvet cloak which was always worn by royalty in every play that boasted regal characters. Then, as Helen of Troy, Martin was led ceremoniously on stage by Mephistopheles. With the eye which was turned from the spectators, Master Kenton winked at him, murmuring out of that corner of his mouth which they could not see, "That should please them! I'll wager not Helen herself looked lovelier!"

Slowly, with grace and regal dignity—for, though flighty, Helen had been a great queen, he reminded himself—Martin walked across the stage and was conscious of the buzz of admiration that stirred the spectators. No hard-won triumph, this one, he was thinking. Helen was the easiest of characters to play if one had the looks: Marlowe had written no speeches for her. He disappeared again behind the screens to await Helen's second entrance. He did not have to listen for a cue, because

Mephistopheles would fetch him once again, so he was free to relax and enjoy a brief rest.

The play was going well, he thought, pleased. And he himself was doing none too ill, with his several parts and the costume changes they involved; not ill at all, considering it was a play with only two short speaking parts for women—neither of which he was playing—and was, therefore, a far from satisfactory play, regarded from his point of view. Though it did offer some good practice for the future, he reflected, since there would be not much longer before his voice broke and he could play no more woman's parts. Well, he had no fear of being unwanted in the company. Unlike some boy players he did not owe his success merely to looks and voice alone. He would, he knew, when the day came, play the hero with as much skill and success and satisfaction as he had played the heroine. Will Kenton—the best player in the company; better even than old Master Banbury—had been training him for two years now against that day. And while he stepped straight from playing women to playing gay young lovers and the like, Crispin and little Robin would be doing their best with the roles which he would have bequeathed them—and failing to achieve a tithe of his success. It was no easy life, there was much hard work, he admitted that. But it was a good life and he would not change it for any other in the world; yet it had been mere chance that had brought him to it. Deliberately Martin turned his mind back to the present. He always preferred not to remember those first seven lonely years which had ended for him on that thrice blessed day when the players had come by, and, struck by the beauty of the unloved orphan, had relieved his harsh foster parents of a burden they had rejoiced to lose.

The grey Franciscan figure appeared beside him to rouse him from his day-dreams. From beneath the cowl Will's face grinned at him. "Come, it's time for their second chance to gape at you. I trust they know how privileged they are!"

They took hands, and with fiendish triumph in this latest step in the downfall of the unfortunate Faustus, Mephistopheles led Helen of Troy from behind the screens; bowing over her hand, as he released it, in a manner more suited to a courtier than an apparent friar.

112

> Was this the face that launched a thousand ships,
> And burnt the topless towers of Ilium? . . .

queried Dr Faustus, in Master Banbury's most ringing tones; and, every inch a queen of ancient days, Helen walked slowly towards him, the first faint traces of a beguiling smile beginning to curve her lips.

And so the play moved on to its grim ending. Abandoned by the Good Angel, to an accompaniment of thunder—cymbals crashed noisily behind the screens—a vainly pleading Faustus was dragged off to hell by two devils—one of them rather small and shrill—whose bloodcurdling howls and fiendish laughter amply compensated for their lack of numbers. Then Chorus, still in the person of the Good Angel, gravely pronounced his final moralizing words: the play was over and, from the applause, an undeniable success.

Of the four who had remained in the castle kitchen only old Samuel had a mind at peace, nodding and snoring on a stool so close beside the fire that it seemed as though he were seeking, on this mild autumn evening, to store up in his twisted, aching old body as much warmth as he might against the icy winter days that lay ahead.

Tom squatted on the straw, thin arms about thin knees, staring at the floor and hearing Simon the puritan, who sat at a table, his greasy, well-thumbed Bible open before him, half reading and half declaiming in his grating voice passages which seemed to him appropriate to the sin of play-acting and the fate of those who concerned themselves with it. Tom felt as though every word were being directed at him, and him alone, because he had wanted so much to see the players.

Her feet shuffling on the flagstones, Mad Meg went up and down the length of the kitchen, singing a plaintive lullaby to her cradled, empty arms. Twelve years before, so Tom had heard the tale told, Meg had been a fair young widow with a son. One day the child had wandered off alone and fallen into the deep mill pool and there been drowned; and from grief Meg had gone out of her mind. She was a good dairymaid, and hardworking, and she harmed no one; but all the while she worked, and whenever her work was done, she would talk or sing quietly to herself without pause—only it was not to herself that she spoke and crooned, but to her child. Sometimes, but rarely, she would remember that the boy was dead, and cry out against the cruel waters of the mill pool.

She was the only person Tom could have named, who had never, by word or deed, caused him hurt. Living in a withdrawn world of her own, she was usually unaware of him and never spoke to him save on those infrequent occasions when the tangible world outside her became, for a little while, as real to her as that other world in her own mind; then she would seek him out as being the youngest of the scullions and warn him with terrifyingly convincing earnestness never to go near the mill pool, lest he should fall in and be drowned.

Hearing her now, he thought—as he had thought before, and more than once—how strange it was that God, Who was said to be good and just, should have permitted a beloved only child to drown, bringing his mother a sorrow that stole her wits away;

while he, Tom, whom no one wanted, lived and flourished to be despised and beaten. Meg's tender lullaby, no less than her sorrow, seemed to Tom to reproach him for living and breathing when her own child was dead and gone. Good Mistress Meg, he implored her in his heart, do not blame me, for today I would so willingly change places with your son.

It is curious how, day in and day out for year after year, one can accept misery, and endure, and exist without hope; and never think to seek a means of escape from one's wretched condition. And then one day there will come but a single instance of a new affliction—perhaps small enough in itself in comparison with its precursors—that can, in a moment, break one, as not all the accumulated and accustomed trials had been able to do. Such an affliction had that day fallen upon Tom; and where before he had, like an animal, accepted tribulation blindly, and endured, he now saw the full extent of the hopelessness of his existence and believed he could endure no longer.

Yet would he find the courage he needed, he wondered, picturing himself stealing from the castle and running, running down the track to the village, and so to the watermill. In imagination he stood on the brink of the pool above the dark water and felt it call to him.

Tomorrow, he promised himself, tomorrow I shall have the courage, and tomorrow I shall be free.

The play being over, the servants began to return to the kitchen, most of them excitedly talking over the evening's entertainment. Tom could not bear to know what those marvels were, which he had missed. Afraid of overhearing of some delight which had been denied to him, he stole away, out of the kitchen and along a poorly lighted passage, caring not where he went so long as he was beyond the reach of the cheerful chattering. His steps soon dragged to a standstill. By this time tomorrow, he thought, the waters of the mill pool would have swallowed him—but he would have not even a Mad Meg to mourn for him. Of a sudden overwhelmingly desolate, he dropped to his knees, covered his face with his hands and burst into tears. Crouched forward he wept brokenheartedly. After some moments, above the sound of his own sobs, he caught the sound of voices. Always wary and over-expectant of blame or punishment, he looked up quickly. Coming towards him along the passage was a small, dark figure, carrying a lighted torch. He heard it speak shrilly and clearly—too clearly for him to have misheard the words which shocked him with swift terror.

"I hope they've thought to give us all a large tankard of ale apiece. Dragging sinners off to hell is thirsty work."

Transfixed with fear, Tom watched the dark figure approach. Too afraid to attempt to fly from it, he crouched against the foot of the wall in the shadows. Suddenly the figure began to skip up and down, flourishing the flaring torch and chanting in bloodcurdling accents, "Dragging sinners off to hell, off to hell, off to hell, dragging sinners off to hell is thirsty work."

The dark figure was perhaps no taller than Tom would have been, had he been standing and not cowering in its path. As it came even nearer, Tom saw by the torchlight that it was pitch black from top to toe; and that upon its head—he was able to see quite plainly now, shock having dammed the flow of his tears—upon its head, dear God protect us, were two horns. Flourishing the torch and still chanting its ghastly song, the creature spun neatly round on its heels three times, setting its own and other shadows to a horrid dancing on the walls; and, as it turned—oh, worse and worse!—Tom could see it had a tail.

At that moment Tom became aware that behind it was a taller, paler figure, which now spoke for the first time. "You imp of Satan, stop jigging about and making such a din, or it's you who'll be picked up and tossed back into hell, where you belong."

The little black devil—for poor Tom had now no doubts as to what the creature was—gave a wail of extreme anguish and cried out, in the most supplicating tones, "Your pardon, your pardon, I beseech you, great master! Look not so fierce on me! Oh, spare me! Ugly hell gape not! I will be good and quiet, I swear I will. See how quiet I am!" Holding the torch high, the devil advanced on tiptoe, with long silent strides, and it was almost upon the terrified Tom before it noticed him in the shadows. With a startled squeal, it retreated. "Oh! There's someone there, on the floor. Look!"

The taller figure came forward. "Bring the torch! Why, it's only a boy, no bigger than you. That's nothing to be scared of."

The torch, held out by the devil, showed Tom's tear-stained face and reddened eyes. "What's wrong? Why do you weep?"

The clear, high voice was like no other that Tom had ever heard. He stared up at the tall being which seemed to tower above him. Slim and straight, all dazzling gold and white in the torchlight: spotless white robe, golden hair encircled by a ring of fire above a serene and lovely face, and, just glimpsed over its shoulders, glowing with gold and rainbow colours—yes, surely those were wings? "You . . . you must be an angel," faltered Tom.

"To be sure I am an angel: and a good angel at that!" The angel smiled at him, and Tom had never dreamt that any face could be so beautiful. Without taking his eyes from the countenance which so graciously looked down on him, he gestured with his hand and asked fearfully, "And that other: what is he?"

The angel's smile deepened and he gave a little, melodious laugh—just such a laugh as one might have expected from an angel, had one ever presumed to imagine an angel laughing—and said, 'Oh, he! He is the blackest and wickedest of all the smaller devils sent to plague mankind. But you have no cause to fear his mischief, for I have overcome him and he is now my slave."

The blackest and wickedest of all the smaller devils made a sound which, in a human being, would have been an exclamation of indignant protest; but which, Tom supposed, must be a devil's way of expressing sorrow for his fate.

The angel spared no glance for the defeated devil, but continued to smile down at Tom. "Did you not see the play, then?" he asked.

Tom shook his head. "No. In the end he would not let me, though he had said I might."

"Who would not let you?"

"Master Walters, my lord's head cook. He's so often cruel and unfair to me. So, too, are many of the others." In a more matter of fact voice, Tom added in explanation, "You see, I'm only Tom Turnspit of the kitchen, so no one's ever kind to me."

"But what of your father and mother, Tom? Are they, also, servants here? And are they not kind?"

"I never had a mother or a father. I'm a foundling."

The angel was silent for a few moments before replying; then he said, "I am sorry. It's a bad thing to be an orphan. I know: for I, too, had no father or mother."

Tom, who had begun to feel reassured by the angel's apparent benevolence, now forgot even more of his fear in surprise at the angel's words. At first he could only stare up in wonder; and then he understood. Of course, how should an angel, begotten in heaven of flame and light and glory, have parents like mortal men? Yet how strange it was that an angel should, like a poor scullion, regret having no parents. But even while he puzzled over this, it came to him that a deficiency which he shared with one of God's glorious angels could be no shame at all. To be in a like condition to an immortal angel, even if only in this one respect, was cause for pride, not shame.

"How old are you?" he heard the angel ask.

"I do not know. No one has ever told me."

"Stand up then, so I may see you." The angel held out a hand to him and Tom wondered whether he dared touch the hand, to kiss it. Timidly he raised his own hand a little way towards the angel's; then, too awed to complete his gesture, was about to draw his hand back when he found it in the angel's grasp and himself being raised to his feet. The angel looked him up and down thoughtfully, then pronounced, "About ten years old, I'd guess." He went on, encouragingly, "That is ten bad years behind you already. You're well past half-way to better days: not many of the bad years remain for you. You'll not be hectored and tormented for ever, you know—though now it may seem so. You'll grow older, and quickly, too: from hour to hour we ripe and ripe. One day you'll find yourself as tall and strong as anyone, with a fine big beard to bristle at them, and a fine deep voice for growling at them. And when that day comes they'll not dare to cross you or to . . . Or to pluck off your beard or call you villain or break your pate across! Indeed, the shoe may well be on the other foot, and it be you who'll be hectoring and tormenting them. Try to remember that, whenever things go ill for you: you'll find it helps, I promise you. And one thing more, and by no means the least: show yourself a little respect and admiration. For the more highly you rate yourself, the more highly others will rate you. Do you think you'll be able to remember so many things without me to prompt you?"

Tom, still awed, but at the same time exhilarated, nodded. "I'll try to remember—always," he whispered.

The angel turned his head to glance over his shoulder. He raised a hand to his left wing and brought it away holding something which he offered to Tom with a friendly, and almost human, chuckle. "A keepsake to aid your memory. Lay it safely by and look at it whenever you need to remind yourself of the good angelic counsel you've been given today."

Reverently Tom took from the angel's outstretched hand a single golden feather, stiff and glittering. Wonderingly he gazed at it.

"Now it must be good night, Thomas Turnspit. Farewell, and good luck to you." The angel snapped his fingers to call the little

black devil who was stifling a wide yawn with the hand that was not holding the torch.

While Tom was yet staring at the golden feather, the angel and the little devil had turned a corner; by the time Tom looked up, not even the light of their torch could be seen. Had it not been for the golden feather he held, they might never have been there, or he might have believed it a dream—or rather, he might, had it not been for both the golden feather and the angel's counsel, which he was never, never going to forget. And it was true: they had been there. A fierce joy suddenly rose in him. God was, after all, good and just, and He had not forgotten him. He had sent him an angel with a message of hope. For poor, slighted Tom Turnspit had He done this. Not to my lord, not to my lady, not to any of their sons or daughters, not to Bible-reading Simon who talked so much of Him, not to Master Bolton nor to Master Walters, and not even to poor, suffering Mad Meg—but to Tom Turnspit had He sent His angel.

Standing there with the feather in his hand, and hope taking root, to grow and blossom, in his heart, Tom promised himself that no one else should ever learn of the favour which had been granted to him alone. It was his own great secret; and so long as it remained inviolate and his alone, so long would he be as strong as—and stronger than—all others who did not share his knowledge and had not been granted a like experience. As for the feather, no eyes but his should ever share the sight of it. He would find a scrap of cloth to wrap about it, he decided, and a length of thread to knot it fast, and he would hang it safely about his neck, an amulet for his protection, and never leave it off.

In a little while he started back for the kitchen, carefully carrying his treasure. His step was firm now and confident, and he walked hopefully towards the future; for, no matter what others might do or say to him now, with his great secret knowledge he, poor Tom Turnspit—no, not poor Tom Turnspit, but God's own chosen Thomas—God's own chosen Thomas was, by His grace, the equal, and more than the equal, of any man alive.

Jack London

Jack London was born in 1876 in San Francisco. He spent his boyhood on the waterfront, went to work in a cannery at the age of fourteen, and became a brawling, drinking troublemaker. In 1904, a year after returning from a trip to the Arctic in a sealing ship, he won first prize in a newspaper story competition. He then entered High School and with hard study passed the entrance examinations for the University of California. But he stayed at the university for only one semester before taking off to join the Klondike gold rush. This was an important period in his life because it provided the material for the stories that were to make him famous.

His first Klondike stories, vivid accounts of the struggle faced by men and dogs to survive in the frozen northern wastes, were collected in *The Son of the Wolf.* His best known work, *The Call of the Wild,* was published three years later in 1903. It describes the adventures of Buck, a pet dog taken from California to the Yukon, where he learns to be brutal in order to survive. After the death of the kind master who befriends him, Buck turns completely savage and becomes the leader of a wolf pack. *White Fang* tells the reverse story of a wolf who is turned into a pet. Although THAT SPOT also concerns a dog in the Yukon, it is, nevertheless, written in a much lighter vein.

Jack London's tales of the northlands were immensely popular and he became firmly established as a best-selling author. The fifty books he wrote between 1900 and 1916 brought him over a million dollars, which he spent as fast as he earned. He died, exhausted and in despair, in 1916.

That Spot

by Jack London

I don't think much of Stephen Mackaye any more, though I used to swear by him. I know that in those days I loved him more than my own brother. If ever I meet Stephen Mackaye again, I shall not be responsible for my actions. It passes beyond me that a man with whom I shared food and blanket, and with whom I mushed over the Chilcoot Trail, should turn out the way he did. I always sized Steve up as a square man, a kindly comrade, without an iota of anything vindictive or malicious in his nature. I shall never trust my judgment in men again. Why, I nursed that man through typhoid fever; we starved together on the headwaters of the Stewart; and he saved my life on the Little Salmon. And now, after the years we were together, all I can say of Stephen Mackaye is that he is the meanest man I ever knew.

We started for the Klondyke in the fall rush of 1897, and we started too late to get over Chilcoot Pass before the freeze-up. We packed our outfit on our backs part way over, when the snow began to fly, and then we had to buy dogs in order to sled it the rest of the way. That was how we came to get that Spot. Dogs were high, and we paid one hundred and ten dollars for him. He looked worth it. I say *looked*, because he was one of the finest-appearing dogs I ever saw. He weighed sixty pounds, and he had all the lines of a good sled animal. We could never make out his breed. He wasn't husky, nor Malemute, nor Hudson Bay; he looked like all of them and he didn't look like any of them; and top of it all he had some of the white man's dog in him, for on one side, in the thick of the mixed yellow-brown-red-and-dirty-white that was his

123

prevailing colour, there was a spot of coal-black as big as a water-bucket. That was why we called him Spot.

He was a good-looker all right. When he was in condition his muscles stood out in bunches all over him. And he was the strongest-looking brute I ever saw in Alaska, also the most intelligent-looking. To run your eyes over him, you'd think he could outpull three dogs of his own weight. Maybe he could, but I never saw it. His intelligence didn't run that way. He could steal and forage to perfection; he had an instinct that was positively gruesome for divining when work was to be done and for making a sneak accordingly, and for getting lost and not staying lost he was nothing short of inspired. But when it came to work, the way that intelligence dribbled out of him and left him a mere clot of wobbling, stupid jelly would make your heart bleed.

There are times when I think it wasn't stupidity. Maybe, like some men I know, he was too wise to work. I shouldn't wonder if he put it all over us with that intelligence of his. Maybe he figured it all out and decided that a licking now and again and no work was a whole lot better than work all the time and no licking. He was intelligent enough for such a computation. I tell you, I've sat and looked into that dog's eyes till the shivers ran up and down my spine and the marrow crawled like yeast, what of the intelligence I saw shining out. I can't express myself about that intelligence. It is beyond mere words. I saw it, that's all. At times it was like gazing into a human soul, to look into his eyes; and what I saw there frightened me and started all sorts of ideas in my own mind of reincarnation and all the rest. I tell you I sensed something big in that brute's eyes; there was a message there, but I wasn't big enough myself to catch it. Whatever it was (I know I'm making a fool of myself)—whatever it was, it baffled me. I can't give an inkling of what I saw in that brute's eyes; it wasn't light, it wasn't colour; it was something that moved, away back, when the eyes themselves weren't moving. And I guess I didn't see it move, either; I only sensed that it moved. It was an expression—that's what it was—and I got an impression of it. No; it was different from a mere expression; it was more than that. I don't know what it was, but it gave me a feeling of kinship just the same. Oh, no, not sentimental kinship. It was, rather, a kinship of equality. Those eyes never pleaded like a deer's eyes. They challenged. No, it wasn't defiance. It was just a calm assumption of equality. And I don't think it was deliberate. My belief is that it was unconscious on his part. It was there because it was there, and it couldn't help shining out. No, I don't mean shine. It didn't shine; it *moved*. I know I'm talking rot, but if you'd looked into that animal's eyes the way I have, you'd understand. Steve was affected the same way I was. Why, I tried to kill that Spot once—he was no good for anything; and I fell down on it. I led him out into the brush, and he came along slow and unwilling. He knew what was going on. I stopped in a likely place, put my foot on the rope, and pulled my big Colt's. And that dog sat down and looked at me. I tell you he didn't plead. He just looked. And I saw all kinds of incomprehensible things moving, yes, *moving*, in those eyes of his. I didn't really see them move; I thought I saw them, for, as I said before, I guess I only sensed them. And I want to tell you right now that it got beyond me. It was like killing a man, a conscious, brave man, who looked calmly into your gun as much as to say, "Who's afraid?" Then, too, the message seemed so near that, instead of pulling the trigger quick, I stopped to see if I could catch the message. There it was, right before me, glimmering all around in those eyes of his. And then it was too late. I got scared. I was trembly all over, and my stomach generated a nervous palpitation that made me seasick. I just sat down and looked at that dog, and he looked at me, till I thought I was going crazy. Do you want to know what I did? I threw down the gun and ran back to camp with the fear of God in my heart. Steve laughed at me. But I noticed that Steve led Spot into the woods, a week later, for the same purpose, and that Steve came back alone, and a little later Spot drifted back, too.

At any rate, Spot wouldn't work. We paid a hundred and ten dollars for him from the bottom of our sack, and he wouldn't work. He wouldn't even tighten the traces. Steve spoke to him the first time we put him in harness, and he sort of shivered, that was all. Not an ounce on the traces. He just stood still and wobbled, like so much jelly. Steve touched him with the whip. He yelped, but not an ounce. Steve touched him again, a bit harder, and he howled—the regular long wolf howl. Then Steve got mad and

125

gave him half a dozen, and I came on the run from the tent.

I told Steve he was brutal with the animal, and we had some words—the first we'd ever had. He threw the whip down in the snow and walked away mad. I picked it up and went to it. That Spot trembled and wobbled and cowered before ever I swung the lash, and with the first bite of it he howled like a lost soul. Next he lay down in the snow. I started the rest of the dogs, and they dragged him along while I threw the whip into him. He rolled over on his back and bumped along, his four legs waving in the air, himself howling as though he was going through a sausage machine. Steve came back and laughed at me, and I apologized for what I'd said.

There was no getting any work out of that Spot; and to make up for it, he was the biggest pig-glutton of a dog I ever saw. On top of that, he was the cleverest thief. There was no circumventing him. Many a breakfast we went without our bacon because Spot had been there first. And it was because of him that we nearly starved to death up the Stewart. He figured out the way to break into our meat-cache, and what he didn't eat, the rest of the team did. But he was impartial. He stole from everybody. He was a restless dog, always very busy snooping around or going somewhere. And there was never a camp within five miles that he didn't raid. The worst of it was that they always came back on us to pay his board bill, which was just, being the law of the land; but it was mighty hard on us, especially that first winter on the Chilcoot, when we were busted, paying for whole hams and sides of bacon that we never ate. He could fight, too, that Spot. He could do everything but work. He never pulled a pound, but he was the boss of the whole team. The way he made those dogs stand around was an education. He bullied them, and there was always one or more of them fresh-marked with his fangs. But he was more than a bully. He wasn't afraid of anything that walked on four legs; and I've seen him march, single-handed, into a strange team, without any provocation whatever, and put the *kibosh* on the whole outfit. Did I say he could eat? I caught him eating the whip once. That's straight. He started in at the lash, and when I caught him he was down to the handle, and still going.

But he was a good-looker. At the end of the first week we sold him for seventy-five dollars to the Mounted Police. They had experienced dog drivers, and we knew that by the time he'd covered the six hundred miles to Dawson he'd be a good sled-dog. I say we *knew*, for we were just getting acquainted with that Spot. A little later we were not brash enough to know anything where he was concerned. A week later we woke up in the morning to the dangdest dog-fight we'd ever heard. It was that Spot come back and knocking the team into shape. We ate a pretty depressing breakfast, I can tell you; but cheered up two hours afterward when we sold him to an official courier, bound in to Dawson with government dispatches. That Spot was only three days in coming back, and, as usual, celebrated his arrival with a rough-house.

We spent the winter and spring, after our own outfit was across the pass, freighting other people's outfits; and we made a fat stake. Also, we made money out of Spot. If we sold him once, we sold him twenty times. He always came back, and no one asked for their money. We didn't want the money. We'd have paid handsomely for any one to take him off our hands for keeps. We had to get rid of him, and we couldn't give him away, for that would have been suspicious. But he was such a fine looker that we never had any difficulty in selling him. "Unbroke," we'd say and they'd pay any old price for him. We sold him as low as twenty-five dollars, and once we got a hundred and fifty for him. That particular party returned him in person, refused to take his money back, and the way he abused us was something awful. He said it was cheap at the price to tell us what he thought of us; and we felt he was so justified that we never talked back. But to this day I've never quite regained all the old self-respect that was mine before that man talked to me.

When the ice cleared out of the lakes and river, we put our outfit in a Lake Bennett boat and started for Dawson. We had a good team of dogs, and of course we piled them on top of the outfit. That Spot was along—there was no losing him; and a dozen times, the first day, he knocked one or another of the dogs overboard in the course of fighting with them. It was close quarters, and he didn't like being crowded.

"What that dog needs is space," Steve said the second day. "Let's maroon him."

127

We did, running the boat in at Caribou Crossing for him to jump ashore. Two of the other dogs, good dogs, followed him; and we lost two whole days trying to find them. We never saw those two dogs again; but the quietness and relief we enjoyed made us decide, like the man who refused his hundred and fifty, that it was cheap at the price. For the first time in months Steve and I laughed and whistled and sang. We were as happy as clams. The dark days were over. The nightmare had been lifted. That Spot was gone.

Three weeks later, one morning, Steve and I were standing on the river-bank at Dawson. A small boat was just arriving from Lake Bennett. I saw Steve give a start, and heard him say something that was not nice and that was not under his breath. Then I looked; and there, in the bow of the boat, with ears pricked up, sat Spot. Steve and I sneaked immediately, like beaten curs, like cowards, like absconders from justice. It was this last that the lieutenant of police thought when he saw us sneaking. He surmised that there were law-officers in the boat who were after us. He didn't wait to find out, but kept us in sight, and in the M. & M. saloon got us in a corner. We had a merry time explaining, for we refused to go back to the boat and meet Spot; and finally he held us under guard of another policeman while he went to the boat. After we got clear of him, we started for the cabin, and when we arrived, there was that Spot sitting on the stoop waiting for us. Now how did he know we lived there? There were forty thousand people in Dawson that summer, and how did he *savve* our cabin out of all the cabins? How did he know we were in Dawson, anyway? I leave it to you. But don't forget what I have said about his intelligence and that immortal something I have seen glimmering in his eyes.

There was no getting rid of him any more. There were too many people in Dawson who had bought him up on Chilcoot, and the story got around. Half a dozen times we put him on board steamboats going down the Yukon; but he merely went ashore at the first landing and trotted back up the bank. We couldn't sell him, we couldn't kill him (both Steve and I had tried), and nobody else was able to kill him. He bore a charmed life. I've seen him go down in a dog-fight on the main street with fifty dogs on top of him, and when they were separated, he'd appear on all his four legs, unharmed, while two of the dogs that had been on top of him would be lying dead.

I saw him steal a chunk of moose-meat from Major Dinwiddie's cache so heavy that he could just keep one jump ahead of Mrs. Dinwiddie's squaw cook, who was after him with an axe. As he went up the hill, after the squaw gave up, Major Dinwiddie himself came out and pumped his Winchester into the landscape. He emptied his magazine twice, and never touched that Spot. Then a policeman came along and arrested him for discharging firearms inside the city limits. Major Dinwiddie paid his fine, and Steve and I paid him for the moose-meat at the rate of a dollar a pound, bones and all. That was what he paid for it. Meat was high that year.

I am only telling what I saw with my own eyes. And now I'll tell you something, also. I saw that Spot fall through a water-hole. The ice was three and a half feet thick, and the current sucked him under like a straw. Three hundred yards below was the big water-hole used by the hospital. Spot crawled out of the hospital water-hole, licked off the water, bit out the ice that had formed between his toes, trotted up the bank, and whipped a big Newfoundland belonging to the Gold Commissioner.

In the fall of 1898, Steve and I poled up the Yukon on the last water, bound for Stewart River. We took the dogs along, all except Spot. We figured we'd been feeding him long enough. He'd cost us more time and trouble and money and grub than we'd got by selling him on the Chilcoot—especially grub. So Steve and I tied him down in the cabin and pulled our freight. We camped that night at the mouth of Indian River, and Steve and I were pretty facetious over having shaken him. Steve was a funny cuss, and I was just sitting up in the blankets and laughing when a tornado hit camp. The way that Spot walked into those dogs and gave them what-for was hair-raising. Now how did he get loose? It's up to you. I haven't any theory. And how did he get across the Klondyke River? That's another facer. And anyway, how did he know we had gone up the Yukon? You see, we went by water, and he couldn't smell our tracks. Steve and I began to get superstitious about that dog. He got on our nerves, too; and, between you and me, we were just a mite afraid of him.

The freeze-up came on when we were at the mouth of Henderson Creek, and we traded him off for two sacks of flour to an outfit that was bound up White River after copper. Now that whole outfit was lost. Never trace nor hide nor hair of men, dogs, sleds, or anything was ever found. They dropped clean out of sight. It became one of the mysteries of the country. Steve and I plugged away up the Stewart, and six weeks afterward that Spot crawled into camp. He was a perambulating skeleton, and could just drag along; but he got there. And what I want to know is who told him we were up the Stewart? We could have gone to a thousand other places. How did he know? You tell me, and I'll tell you.

No losing him. At the Mayo he started a row with an Indian dog. The buck who owned the dog took a swing at Spot with an axe, missed him, and killed his own dog. Talk about magic and turning bullets aside—I, for one, consider it a blamed sight harder to turn an axe aside with a big buck at the other end of it. And I saw him do it with my own eyes. That buck didn't want to kill his own dog. You've got to show me.

I told you about Spot breaking into our meat-cache. It was nearly the death of us. There wasn't any more meat to be killed, and meat was all we had to live on. The moose had gone back several hundred miles and the Indians with them. There we were. Spring was on, and we had to wait for the river to break. We got pretty thin before we decided to eat the dogs, and we decided to eat Spot first. Do you know what that dog did? He sneaked. Now how did he know our minds were made up to eat him? We sat up nights laying for him, but he never came back, and we ate the other dogs. We ate the whole team.

And now for the sequel. You know what it is when a big river breaks up and a few billion tons of ice go out, jamming and milling and grinding. Just in the thick of it, when the Stewart went out, rumbling and roaring, we sighted Spot out in the middle. He'd got caught as he was trying to cross up above somewhere. Steve and I yelled and shouted and ran up and down the bank, tossing our hats in the air. Sometimes we'd stop and hug each other, we were that boisterous, for we saw Spot's finish. He didn't have a chance in a million. He didn't have any chance at all. After the ice-run, we got into a canoe and paddled down to the Yukon, and down the Yukon to Dawson, stopping to feed up for a week at the cabins at the mouth of Henderson Creek. And as we came in to the bank at Dawson, there sat that Spot, waiting for us, his ears pricked up, his tail wagging, his mouth smiling, extending a hearty welcome to us. Now how did he get out of that ice? How did he know we were coming to Dawson, to the very hour and minute, to be there on the bank waiting for us?

The more I think of that Spot, the more I am convinced that there are things in this world that go beyond science. On no scientific grounds can that Spot be explained. It's psychic phenomena, or mysticism, or something of that sort, I guess, with a lot of Theosophy thrown in. The Klondyke is a good country, I might have been there yet, and become a millionaire, if it hadn't been for Spot. He got on my nerves. I stood him for two years all together, and then I guess my stamina broke. It was the summer of 1899 when I pulled out. I didn't say anything to Steve. I just sneaked. But I fixed it up all right. I wrote Steve a note, and enclosed a package of "rough-on-rats," telling him what to do with it. I was worn down to skin and bone by that Spot, and I was that nervous that I'd jump and look around when there wasn't anybody within hailing distance. But it was astonishing the way I recuperated when I got quit of him. I got back twenty pounds before I arrived in San Francisco, and by the time I'd crossed the ferry to Oakland I was my old self again, so that even my wife looked in vain for any change in me.

Steve wrote to me once, and his letter seemed irritated. He took it kind of hard because I'd left him with Spot. Also, he said he'd used the "rough-on-rats", per directions, and that there was nothing doing. A year went by. I was back in the office and prospering in all ways—even getting a bit fat. And then Steve arrived. He didn't look me up. I read his name in the steamer list, and wondered why. But I didn't wonder long. I got up one morning and found that Spot chained to the gate-post and holding up the milkman. Steve went north to Seattle, I learned, that very morning. I didn't put on any more weight. My wife made me buy him a collar and tag, and within an hour he showed his gratitude by killing her pet Persian cat. There is no getting rid of that Spot. He will be with me until I die, for he'll never die. My appetite is not so good since he arrived, and my wife says I am looking peaked.

Last night that Spot got into Mr. Harvey's hen-house (Harvey is my next door neighbour) and killed nineteen of his fancy-bred chickens. I shall have to pay for them. My neighbours on the other side quarrelled with my wife and then moved out. Spot was the cause if it. And that is why I am disappointed in Stephen Mackaye. I had no idea he was so mean a man.

Judith Wright

Judith Wright was born in 1915 near Armidale, New South Wales. She spent much of her girlhood on her parents' sheep station and, because there were no schools nearby, received her first education through the New South Wales Correspondence School. After graduating from Sydney University, she spent a year in Europe. When she returned to Australia, she worked as a stenographer, a secretary, a statistician and an agriculturalist. She now lives at North Tamborine in southern Queensland.

She is best known for her poetry, being recognised as Australia's leading contemporary poet, but her stories are also of outstanding quality. They are not, however, written in what many people falsely think of as a "poetic" style: there are no involved descriptions or exaggerated images. Instead, her prose is simple, direct and compelling.

"Outside the lighted window, something moved. Eyes watched, a hand went out and very quietly touched the window-bars; then after a while, a shadow moved round the house, from locked door to locked door. . . ."

The above extract comes from *The River and the Road,* one of her novels for young people. It is set in Australia in 1859 – the time of horse-drawn coaches and gold prospecting – and tells the strange story of a man who cannot forget the dark, unjust days of his youth and returns to seek his revenge in the small township along the Great North Road to Sydney.

Two other books for young people, which are equally absorbing, are *Kings of the Dingoes* and *Range the Mountains High.*

The Nature of Love, the collection of short stories from which HOLIDAYS and THE ANT LION are taken, is intended more for adult readers, as is her historical memoir *The Generations of Men.*

Holidays

by Judith Wright

Toby ran down the steep, guttered road from the shop, half-blind with tears. He was crying so much that he caught his foot in a root that ran out into the road from Ferguson's fig-tree and barked a knee and his chin on the hot gravel. As it was impossible to cry louder than he had been, he now fell quite silent, and limping home, only sobbed. But the tears fell in a flood.

Eleanor and John were pulling pickets off the cottage-fence, behind the coral-tree, when he came through the back gate. They wanted a secret entrance to foil the plots of Savage's Gang, who had waited for them yesterday evening in the dark and caught them coming home from Long Beach, pelting them disagreeably with pieces of dead crab. Eleanor was just going to ask Toby whether he had eaten all his chocolate frog already, when she noticed that his heart was broken; and as always at the sight of his dreadful babyish tears, her blood sprang up in rage against the world.

"What's happened, Toby? What is it?"

"They took it," Toby at last managed to articulate.

"They took your frog? Who did?" But Eleanor knew already; and meeting John's eye she took out her handkerchief and tried to repair Toby's face, which as John said was all slobbered up.

"You should have hit them," John told Toby, quite meaninglessly, since Toby at five was scarcely to be considered a match for Savage's Gang, whose four members were all over the age of nine. What John meant, however, as Eleanor understood, was really that John himself at eight, was not a match for them either, and felt himself and Toby inferior beings.

135

"And there ought to have been a penny change," John continued. "Have you got that?"

"They took it," wept Toby.

"Then they're thieves," Eleanor said. To take chocolate frogs was one thing; pennies, as they had all been taught, were quite another. "Savages *and* thieves. Now," she went on, casting about for some way to change Toby's expression, which, like the look of a rabbit she had once wickedly released from a trap, made her feel quite powerless with misery, "come inside and I'll give you a wash. And a lump of sugar. Auntie's asleep in the front garden."

"Don't want any sugar." Toby, rejecting all kindnesses, staggered alone to the steps and crawled up them on all fours, to emphasize his feelings. Unwashed, he vanished under his bed, where he would lie, Eleanor expected, till lunch-time.

She left him in silence and went back to where John was moodily pushing a loose nail backwards and forwards through the fence.

"It was Pat Malone and Jimmy Woodser," he said. "I just saw them going up to Murphy's tossing the penny."

"They're going fishing this afternoon out to the Cape," Eleanor said. "John, did you bring your catapult?"

He looked at her doubtfully. That catapult. He was not supposed to have it at all; a specially strong and valuable one, it had inflicted fatal damage on the red rooster just before they had left home, signalising John's final recovery from measles. But he had secretly stolen it back from the cupboard drawer . . .

"Yes," he said at last, deciding that for once Eleanor was to be trusted. "But what's the good? If they come after me, I can't run as fast as them; and I don't want to lose it."

"They won't come after you if they don't know who you are," Eleanor said. "We'll ambush them on the road to the Cape. In the marsh. We can duck down in the bushes and they'll never find us."

John's attitude to the enterprise altered. This was certainly an idea. The Cape road ran out through a matted wilderness of heath and banksia scrub, thorny and thick-growing. No one went that way except occasional fishermen, and there were no tracks through the dense waist-high stuff. One could certainly lose oneself in it very effectively, even from hardened locals like Pat

136

Malone and Jimmy Woodser (whose names, incidentally, were gang-conferred and not given by baptism).

But he looked at Eleanor with distaste still. "You're a girl," he accused. "You'll do something silly."

"You will, more likely," Eleanor said. "Now go and look for good stones. I'd better wait about till Auntie wakes up."

It was exasperatingly difficult to induce Toby to go with Auntie on her visit to the Misses Angus, instead of coming out to the Cape road. No one must have even a hint that they were going that way, and it was consequently impossible to tell Toby why he was being jettisoned. Even Auntie, usually anxious to keep "poor little Toby" near her, mildly begged Eleanor to take him, since his rage at the thought of an afternoon with the Anguses was so evident. The Anguses, health faddists, never ate cake or biscuits; their parsley-sandwiched tea-table was shunned by everyone below the age of dieting. But the surreptitious promise of another chocolate frog in the morning finally sent him sulking off.

To deceive possible spies, Eleanor and John left the cottage by the secret gap in the fence, which gave on to a sandy gully down which one could traverse to the beach. Crossing it with every precaution, they struck inland into the fringe of the heathy scrub.

"Damn," said John, "we shouldn't be wearing shorts." The hard, sharp little leaves and wiry twigs stung bitterly; a series of hot scents went up from the crushed plants as they fought their way through.

Half a mile out, they found themselves at the edge of the white sand-strip that was the Cape road. No one was in sight, but John, prowling on hands and scratched knees, announced the tracks of bare feet. "This is Pat," he explained oracularly, "because his are the biggest. This little one is Jimmy; and this one must be Wood-and-Water Joey. And this one"—his voice shook a little—"must be Speed Savage. I didn't think he'd be going."

"Get *him*," Eleanor suggested. "If he gets one good crack, all the rest will run."

"H'm." John examined his shanghai and looked into his bag of stones. "I think it might have perished a bit," he warned Eleanor, "in all this time. It might break or something." He by no means had Eleanor's faith in his aim and presence of mind.

The sun balanced on three rays above a cloud; flights of green-leek lorikeets screamed overhead on the way to the box-scrub at the Cape.

"Suppose you hide here," Eleanor suggested. "I'll go further up, so that when the stone hits them and they start to go after you, I can throw another from behind. That'll confuse them. Then both of us dodge back alone as quick as we can, and try to keep the bushes from moving as we go."

Hidden a few yards from the quiet road, Eleanor waited. Nothing happened at all. She watched the light gradually yellowing on the bulk of the hills at the Cape, and the mote-filled rays beginning to strike horizontally across the marsh. Mouse-like birds, sharp-beaked, hopped in the dwarf banksias; a honey-eater clung to the tall flower-stem of a grass-tree; a sharp-leaved shrub flowered near her with a vivid scent of honey. At last voices began, coming nearer down the road. She risked one glance from behind a tuft and dropped down again. It was the Gang, all four of them.

How was John feeling, she wondered? It suddenly occurred to her with force that she had led him into frightful danger. Suppose he did not get away? She began to picture the scene, imagining every kind of catastrophe. She gripped the two stones in her pocket with a kind of anguish. "This one is for Toby," she said to herself, with a vague recollection of old tales of battle, "and this one is for John."

The voices drew nearer, engaged in the embroidery of some boastful yarn, passed, went on. Eleanor knelt, gripping her stones. A long time seemed to pass, so long that at last she stood up. There was a far-off shout, and she dropped down so quickly that a heath-branch scratched her. Desperately she crawled forward, parallel to the road, knowing the bushes must be swaying above her, and finding a small clear track to the road, she hurried crouching along it and peered through a banksia.

Silence had succeeded the shout; on the road, as far as she could see, nothing was visible.

She waited there until her knees began to cramp, then boldly stood up again. The marsh stretched away in all directions, dark and quiet in the yellow light; the road was quite empty. The battle,

if there had been one, seemed to have left the neighbourhood; but she did not dare call out to John, in case the Savage Gang were waiting somewhere nearby for a betraying movement.

She dropped down prudently, and began to worm her way rapidly back through the scrub by a new route close to the mangroves. She thought anxiously of John. Had he been overpowered and left for dead somewhere, never to be found in the marsh scrub? The afternoon seemed painfully inconclusive; her wish for revenge had somehow disappeared.

It was in an open sandy patch near the mangroves that she

found the Christmas-bells. Thousands of them, it seemed, had just burst into bloom, red and yellow like wax flowers, like something in a shop made specially for Christmas. And this was all the more poignant since nowhere else, she knew, had they come into flower yet—not in the big patch where everybody picked, nor even in the special early patch under Macdonald's. Forgetting everything, she picked and wandered.

It was almost dark when she reached home, and Auntie was inclined to wail and reproach, but the Christmas-bells explained everything. John was lying on his bed reading, while Toby industriously tried to roller-skate with his feet in two trucks of his train.

"Come outside." She dragged John fiercely off his bed. "What happened? Didn't you get any of them?

"I got old Wood-and-Water," John boasted. "Right in the backside. Didn't you hear him shout?"

"Oh, good man! But what happened then? I couldn't see a thing anywhere."

"I don't know," John said. He seemed as doubtful as she was. "I just made for home."

"They must have hidden, or gone back through the scrub." She was disappointed that there had been no battle. All that bloody scene she had imagined—it had evaporated completely. Even if Wood-and-Water had been hurt, he still did not know it was revenge.

All the emotion of that painful journey through the scratchy scrub had cleared off like smoke, leaving her flat and lacklustre. Perhaps the stone had not even hit Wood-and-Water. She began to doubt it. That shout had not sounded like a shout of pain; and now John's voice rang false in her ears.

'You didn't really hit him, did you?"

"Well!" he shouted. But he was an honest lieutenant. "I didn't think the stone had got that far," he confessed.

"He thought it was a wallaby in the bushes," she mocked. "They all chased off into the scrub thinking they were after a wallaby."

"Perhaps." But John had been pushed too far. He grew haughty. "A lot of use you were, anyway. Now, let me finish this chapter, can't you? It's nearly tea-time."

Toby skated out on to the verandah. He had tied the trucks to his feet with Eleanor's best hair-ribbons.

"You beastly little boy," she cried, and with an accuracy that surprised her, she knocked him down the steps.

Toby in bed, tea over, the crickets shouting up the full moon outside the window, she picked her Christmas-bells out of the tub and began to arrange them in a series of cracked vases left behind by the cottages's former occupants. Tomorrow she would take them round to everyone—to Mrs. Hatrick, to Joan and Betty at the shop.

"How clever you were to find them," she said to herself. "Oh, well, I just thought there might be some, away out there, so I went exploring . . ."

141